What Readers are Saying about

The Confessions of Adam

Whoever thought biblical fiction lacked creativity has not read
The Confessions of Adam. Debut novelist David J. Marsh creates
an on-the-edge of your seat adventure that transports the reader
deep into the heart of Adam. Highly recommended.

~Best selling novelist, DiAnn Mills, author of
***Fatal Strike*(Tyndale)**

The Confessions of Adam by David J. Marsh is thought-provoking
exploration of the possibilities--oh, the possibilities!--of what
is left unsaid in the life of Adam. Though obviously a work of
fiction, and uniquely told to a scribe who needs this story as
much as any of us, it is no less powerful in its ability to transport
us into the world Adam might have known before, during, and
after the moments recorded in Scripture. Emotionally gripping
and rich with meaning for our lives these thousands of years
later, *The Confessions of Adam* has become one of my must-read
recommendations.

~Cynthia Ruchti, award-winning author of 30+ books

The Confessions of Adam is a nuanced and illuminating debut,
a story about a story and a storyteller. David Marsh has the
audacity to give us a new version of Genesis, and (thank God!)
he also has the skill to do it, re-imagining a world we thought
we knew.

~Ben H. Winters, award-winning author of *Golden State*

Apocalypse everywhere one looks today, it seems. Zombie
hordes, alien invasions, climates collapsing. So that's why David
J. Marsh's pristine debut novel, *The Confessions of Adam*, turns
these end times inside out with this brand spanking new take on
Genesis, literally fleshing out the Ur-ist of Urtexts. Here, Adam
is naming names as he enters, for all of us, the great forgetting
of Eden. And yet even Gen contains the heartbreaking
Revelation—spoiler alert! -

Apocalypse. Yes, the detailed fall from grace and that disgraced Hope caught in Pandora's box of Evil. But that is another story, and this, this one is the story you start with.

~**Michael Martone author of**
Brooding and The Moon Over Wapakoneta

Creative. Compassionate. Compelling. David Marsh poignantly captures the regrets and triumphs of the human condition by telling the story of Adam. If you've ever speculated about what it might have been like to walk and talk with God, or how long it took to name the animals, or what the first man thought when he saw the first woman, or how they handled the birth of their first child, you'll find this book a fascinating read. It will draw you in and capture your imagination from the very beginning. When *The Confessions of Adam* ended, I was wishing for more.

~**Carol Kent, Speaker and Author**
He Holds My Hand: Experiencing God's
Presence and Protection(Tyndale)

The Confessions of Adam

The Confessions of Adam

With Oren of Susa

A Novel

David J. Marsh

Bold Vision Books
PO Box 2011
Friendswood, Texas 77549

Published in the United States of America.
Published by Bold Vision Books, PO Box 2011,
Friendswood, Texas 77549 www.boldvisionbooks.com
Published in association with literary agent: Joelle
Delbourgo Associates, Inc., 101 Park St, Montclair, NJ.
07042

Dedication

For CKM
… she is a gift from The Maker.

And In Memory of
Robert Ernest Marsh,
who gave me the love of books,

and

Marlene Joyce Schaiper Marsh Crump,
who gave me the love for what they could hold.

For He Himself knows our frame;
He is mindful that we are but dust.
~David, psalmist, c. 990 BC

The pain I feel now is the happiness
I had before. That's the deal.
~C.S. Lewis

Table of Contents

Oren of Susa: Scribe's Preface

My signet ring cracks against the boy's skull. The sound echoes from the leafy, towering hardwoods on the far riverbank. The boy cries out but quickly hushes himself, burying his face in the crook of his arm. The other boys lift their heads and peer out of the corners of their eyes as they wade deeper into the tallest reeds. They don't risk a stare.

"To the bells!"

I grab the wrist of the whimpering child and pull him from the river's edge up onto the bank and over to the basket of bells. His stringy brown hair is stuck to his forehead in a sweaty paste. He wipes his nose on his sleeve, his face slick with tears.

"Put them on like the others," I say, releasing my grip.

The boy's arm drops to his side. Amat, an older student and this year's assistant, steps over to where the boy and I stand. I let him take over and return to my spot in the shade.

Three seasons back a failure just like this cost one boy his life. He did not see the water snake and his bells were in the basket, rather than strapped to him where they could jingle to startle and repel. Like this boy, he had been anxious to wade into the cool river in the heat of the afternoon. He died, collapsed in knee-deep water, his face submerged, his small fist wrapped around the last reed he had grasped.

Amat gently helps the sniffling boy tie his soaked smock up in a knot at his back and wraps a strand of bells just above each of the child's elbows and knees. This done, he pats the boy's head—no doubt a knot has risen from my reprimand—and ushers the child to the river's edge, watching over him as he eases into the water and wades back in among the other boys.

I watch Amat do this and I don't stop him or think anything of it. I was once a scribe's assistant. I know the foolish boy's father lines the purse of the assistant for doling out such coddling.

From my perch in the shade I watch. The boys' heads bob in silence as they bend and rummage in the muck with their stubby fingers, their bells tinkling. One is standing and dancing about. He needs to urinate. He will wait until we're done.

The sunlight of evening sparkles on the River Shapur as the new class of boys, each in their sixth year of life, searches for reeds among the thick grasses. Just upstream, horses' hooves clap against the worn timbers of the bridge into and out of Susa. Ox carts pass flatwagons. Yoke chains sound as the drivers holler to their teams or lob greetings to one another. The afternoon markets have closed and the farmers are returning home under a cloudless sky, their cartage empty but for firewood and fresh meat. I delight in the sounds and sights of this place. Since birth they have filled my ears and eyes.

This is my forty-seventh season as scribe. Forty-seven springs I have stood in this spot and listened to these bells. They come to me as walking babies—dull and stupid boys, lacking discipline. They leave me far greater men than their fathers will ever be.

They learn at the most respected tablet house in the valley, or the entire river land, for that matter. By their thirteenth year those who have not fled out of weakness will be full scribes. They will be in far-off villages, apprenticed in the laws or with market-keepers. They will take with them their share of my reputation. They will benefit from what I offer for the rest of their lives. They have not the slightest idea. I give them all that I have, and in return I receive only stares and gold coins that I must lean close to count, due to my failing eyesight.

Pulling reeds is where they start. Each lesson—from pointing the reed and cutting the clay to spacing with care each jot and tittle—is built on this one, on the ability to do this simple task as instructed. Every step is a test. Every action has a purpose.

So far, a mound of reeds, the girth of a muskmelon, lies in the grass by the basket. I estimate there to be thirty or thirty-two stalks, though the muddy, fresh-torn roots make my inspection difficult. Each stalk must measure the thickness of the thumb of the boy who harvested it. But directions are not always followed. About half of these reeds will be too thin and flimsy or too thick and woody and will be left to dry and throw in the fire.

Amat comes over and stands beside me. He is a head taller than I and thin. His hair in its youthful ebony contrasts with my scalp of short, gray scrub.

"There must be at least two times this number to afford each boy a styli and a spare for the first week's copying," I remind him.

"Yes, Master Oren. I will see to it."

Amat steps atop a boulder that sits at the edge of the river's current.

"Work faster," he calls. "Encourage the boy next to you. You don't want to be walking back to the village and to your homes in the dark, do you? Better an aching back now."

The threat of darkness visibly quickens each boy's pace. They are young, their fears simple and deep.

I think ahead to tomorrow, the instruction in cutting the reeds, the trimming of the straws to a point. Amat will sharpen the knives this evening. I've seen blood trickling down a boy's arm a thousand times, the knife slipping into one small thumb after another. But even so, it nearly makes my stomach spill.

Two of the boys who have been rewarded for their diligence trim the stalks to the length of a forearm, and wrap the bottoms of the reeds in thick bolts of felt, making bundles of muddy roots. They lay these in the bottom of the basket and the strands of bells are piled in on top by each boy in single file. Finally, the two boys lift, each on an end of the basket, and turn to lead our procession back toward the village.

The bridge is quiet now, so we climb up to the road to cross the river. The sky's two great lights have taken their places, one coloring the horizon as it leaves and the other hanging in crisp white at our backs. The shuffle of the boys' feet, the rattle of the basket, and an occasional whisper are the only sounds—save the call of a pair of crows. I look down the long, straight road as we walk. Smoke rises from the first evening fires and the watchman's torches have begun to flicker in the cooling dusk. It is then, as we clear the bridge, that I see him.

A messenger.

I know him by his withered leg. He comes toward us at something between a hobble and a limp. He lurches to one side in such a way that it seems he might tip over. He is one of the public stable of messengers for hire. The boys break into a noisy chatter as he nears. I remain at the back of the class. As we meet him it amuses me to watch him dodging his way between the boys, each looking up at him, their faces in a stew of expectation and qualm. I call a halt just as he gets to me. The boys fall silent and we all stop moving at once.

"A strange—." The messenger pauses, waiting, wheezing, finally catching his breath. "A stranger at tab-tablet house."

Arms draped over his walking rod, his tongue flaps and clicks in his dry hole of a mouth. He has two browning yellow teeth. One hangs in the corner of his mouth and the other pushes up from the center like an old stump.

"Go on," I say, stirring the air with my hand, anxious to be done with him. "Did you not get a name from this visitor?"

The boys gather around as if at a fight, sizing up their wager.

"It is a man," says the messenger.

"Can you describe this man?"

"He is alone, old. A throng follows along behind him as he walks. Everyone stares at him."

The messenger pauses again, apparently empty of details. I am not empty of questions.

"Do you recognize this visitor?"

"No. He is common enough, but he is like a camel, all knees and limbs."

"Then he is not that common."

"No. I must say. Not that common."

"So he's waiting at the tablet house now?"

"Yes. But he will come back within the next two days if you are not at the tablet house in a short time."

"Fine. Anything else?"

"If I may, I—"

"Yes?"

The messenger stands in front of me, his eyes fixed on my purse.

Messengers are an odd company of men, milling about in the market, without skill, most of them with some manner of warped or missing body part. Such jobs of message carrying feed them well enough. Custom would be to toss him the coins to buy two duck eggs or enough wheat to fill his palms when cupped together. And I might follow the custom but I have a higher calling. The boys are watching. They need prompting to work hard and avoid a wasted life. So I give the messenger nothing. I make no move to grasp my bulging purse. As he stares my resolve is set. Such broken apes as this are better off dead. Alms only prolong their dreary state.

"If he remains when you return, tell him that I will see him mid-day tomorrow."

"Yes, and I will. As you have said." The messenger would do anything I ask, holding ever tighter to his hope for some payment.

If the visitor chooses never to return, so much the better. It is happening more and more. People have been stopping at the tablet house every day, sometimes two and three times a day. They ask me if I might like to buy a cow or a pig or a goat. When I say no they say, "I could bring milk or a sack of wool to you once a week?" Others ask if I would like furniture built or new glass in my windows. Perhaps my roof needs repairing? Some of them ask if I can spare a few coins to aid local orphans, or if I'd like to purchase one as a servant.

Another visitor is not welcome, nor is he news. I only offer to see him because I am as curious as anyone else — a table maker doesn't have a crowd following him.

The ring of boys opens into a crescent as the messenger gives up on my purse, bows, and dips to one side, turning and easing down the riverbank. He plunges his face into the water and sucks madly, his jowls and chin dripping as he surfaces. A bit of scum hangs from his chin. Pulling himself back up to the road, he makes his way ahead of us again, toward the village.

I look at the basket of reeds the boys are carrying and I think of this poor half-cripple's mind — bundles of muddy roots, bundles of muddy roots.

Dusk is fully upon us. I call out. "Mind your pace boys, lift your feet."

Amat has pulled the cot out of the closet and is napping in the quiet of the lecture room. The boys are all at home or at their parents' shops eating, thinking about anything but the letters. These first weeks with a new class always make me feel like a wet nurse. So little is about the letters. All is about keeping their attention, tending to their little spirits. Soon I'll make one or two of the boys an example—pulled to the front of the class, their smocks lifted and their bare backsides blistered with a strip of leather. The weeks will then become much easier.

Hanging overhead, the midday sun feels close. Even though I know the heat will have driven many to the twin rivers to bathe, I walk through the crowded market toward the River Dez. The water's edge comes into sight and it is more than I thought. Half the population of Susa has decided to go for a bath. Piles of filthy clothing dot the riverbank at the end of the street—hats, linen tunics, and overshirts lay in loose bundles next to sandals, their straps flung in the dirt. Any reeds that once grew here have been long since stomped out. The water churns with children screaming and laughing, kicking and splashing in litters of a dozen or more from one bank to the other. Their mothers stand close together, breasts sagging, gossiping in huddles at the edges of the action. A few fathers keep watch—standing like towers here and there—arms folded over their hairy chests, water up to their pale buttocks. The current appears nearly stopped as it piles up against the teeming mass of sweaty flesh.

I will enter upstream of this mayhem, for downstream the water is thick and cloudy, stagnant. The crowd bustles around me as I slowly make my way. Some of them look at me and nod, most ignore me altogether, their arms full of clothing and food or small children. A trio of dogs lap at the edge of the water—lifting their heads and shuffling this way or that to avoid the steps of bathers. The nearest dog starts to cut into my path. I kick it out of my way, causing it to stumble and tip on its side in the mud. The beast is no dirtier for the wear. Further up the riverbank I find my spot under a nearly dead cedar. I drop my slippers and drape my smock over a bare limb, the bark worn smooth from my use.

I descend the bank until the water rises to my ankles. The sun on my back feels as if it could bake me like clay. All naked bodies, once they reach the age of mine, have ugly shapes, bulges, and flab in one place or another. Always skin and bones loosely cobbled together, starting with a head and usually ending with feet. I am a daytime bather. The young bathe at night, when there are fires on the riverbank and barrels of drink. Under the light of the stars, there are no bulges or flab, only muscles and curves. Toward dawn they lay on the bank in pairs, threes, fours, a few moments spent entwined together before sunrise.

I remember such nights. How I found my way from one girl to another, the light of the bonfire casting its shadow. And I remember finding her. How we enjoyed our youth night after night, she and I, off away from the others. But this joy is long faded. The scab of losing her is thick, like dried sap over a split branch in late autumn. And the memory of the touch of her warm, soft skin only reminds me that my loins have turned to flab.

I step toward the center of the river and pause—the water suddenly cool as it meets my underbody. I lie back and float downstream, my arms and legs working with the current. I feel the water against the top of my head.

Voices echo from across the water. The sun sparkles in the current and my mind wanders to my sabbatical. With some direction, which I've already begun to give, Amat could take the class this harvest while I slip away for a couple of months before the heart of the winter. Or I could turn the house over to him for much longer and avoid altogether this new class of boys—the stench of their sweaty bodies in the heat of the afternoon. I could simply walk away and return when I saw fit.

Wading against the current I step back up the riverbank and under the cedar. Chilled a bit there in the shade I relieve myself against a milkweed that has grown up along the trunk. My thoughts turn to food. I step back into my slippers and wrap myself in my smock.

On my way back to the tablet house I stop at a fruit vendor for yogurt and nuts, as well as a pomegranate—Amat's daily request. I am too good to him.

Some time away. Perhaps I could travel, maybe to the sea. The poetry I worked on last year is an unruly mess. I can hardly call it poetry. It is meant to be an epic verse about my life as a scribe. But like an afternoon with the boys it is lifeless and overly familiar. I cannot decide which is the greater bore—to read what I have written so far or to write some more.

Goods in hand, I continue toward the tablet house. The chalky dust is already layering itself on my feet, and the sun has quickly dried my scalp. I am nearly within sight of the house when Amat walks up to me, anxious for my attention.

"Master Oren, the visitor has returned." His voice carries a girlish brightness, a chirp that grates on my ear over the din of the busy market. My lack of response spurs him on. "The visitor, the one the messenger told us about last evening."

"Yes, Amat. I remember. Are any of the boys back for the afternoon session?"

"No. Not yet. I have let the visitor in to sit in the lecture room. There is a small crowd in the street. It is just as the messenger said." Amat folds his hands tight at his chin as he speaks.

"Amat, what is it?"

He steps close. "I think it may be him."

"Whom?"

"I think it may be the Created One."

I squint into the hot sun and look up, straight into Amat's wide eyes. The boy's imagination is making a fool of him.

"What makes you think such a thing?"

"The noise in the crowd. I overheard several of the old women say it." Amat stands to my side and takes my elbow as if to lead me on to the house. "Besides, he is old and very tall. He is impossible to ignore. And his features, they suggest having lived much."

The marketplace crowd is too heavy. Amat releases my elbow and takes the lead, splitting the crowd as I come along behind him. In among the market stalls and craftsmen's workshops, the tablet house comes into view. Its arched grass roof is set atop its plain rectangular frame. The front door is set in oak beams, as are the windows, all of which face the street. Amat turns to me. "Look at them!" Indeed, a small crowd has gathered at the door and is slowly growing. "They were following him. Word is spreading."

As I approach, the nearest ones look at me as if I am hosting one of their gods. I hate their attention, their pushing in around me. Their foul hot breath and stares repulse and unnerve me. Their broad expectant grins and filthy teeth—I am not one of them.

"Go home! Haven't you anything better to do?"

They only stare more, as if I am not Oren, the same plain-faced literate they've seen padding along these dirt streets their entire lives.

"Maybe you'll learn to mark your name if you stay long enough!"

None of them say a word. I stand behind Amat as he grasps the latch to open the door. He looks back at me as if to ask if I am ready. I urge him on and he enters ahead of me. He steps in and looks around the room twice and then a third time. The house is empty. The door still hanging open, one of the crowd steps in. "He has gone to get food and is coming back soon!"

I turn and grab the man, pushing him back outside. He stumbles into the murmuring mass. Knocking several of them aside he loses his balance and falls. I close the door, locking it.

I put our food on the desk, remove my slippers, and rinse my feet in the foot bath. Amat steps to the window.

"The people are excited," he says.

I sit at my desk to eat. "They lead drab lives, Amat. They are not excited, they are longing—like blind men for some bit of light."

The yogurt tastes of honey and cloves. I toss a few almonds into it and watch Amat fetch a knife for his pomegranate from the cutting block in the corner. He returns to the window, his back in a studied hunch. I can hear the buzzing of the crowd rising and falling, rising again, waiting for the visitor to return. These people need a purpose. My purpose is to enjoy my midday meal. I walk to the door and jerk it open. It looks like some have left to look for him, but many have stayed behind. Startled, they jump away and scatter into the street. But as soon as I close the door and lock it again they return like flies.

In disgust I sit back down and pour a few extra almonds out onto my desk. I settle back and eat.

Amat looks over at me. "Listen, Master. They have grown quiet."

He is right. It is as if the crowd has left. Only a couple of muffled voices carry through the wall on the thick afternoon air. I know I have only a short while before the boys begin to return for the second session. I sit back, put my feet up on the lecture desk, and begin to relax. In the quiet a drowse comes over me.

Three knocks sound against the door. I sit back up slowly and move the yogurt from my lap to the desk. Amat looks toward the entry way and then over at me.

"Go ahead," I say.

Amat steps around and down the short hall to attend the door as I slipper my feet and stand at my desk, smoothing my smock for business.

A flash of sunlight, noise, and hot air fills the entry way.

"Come in please, sir," I hear Amat say.

There is shuffling of feet and the door shuts.

A moment of silence, then Amat again. "One moment please."

Amat steps from around the corner and hands me a small remnant of lambskin — a traveling note. Few visitors have traveling notes. I haven't seen one in years. It is a very old practice.

I look down at the note pinched between my forefinger and thumb. I am surprised to see that it is not made of words nor is it signed by any ruler or overseer. On it is a drawing of a tree. Etched and lightly brushed, the tree looks as if you could lift it off the skin. I can see nests, pockets of grass nestled in nooks and branches, tiny beaks and heads pop up and down as the skin shifts under my gaze. Ripe fruit clusters, dangling stems burdened by the weight. Each leaf is shaded such that it seems to flutter in a sunny evening breeze.

Below this, in a flowing, curling scrawl appear the only words: Adam of Eden.

I turn back toward Amat and motion for him to bring the visitor in.

I look down again at the note and think of the myths. The Created One. Man of Men. The Beginner. He goes by many names. Only the very oldest in the village claim to have ever seen the man, though everyone has an opinion of him. The tales I have heard are that he is not living in this region, that he is living near the sea to the north. This is only talk. If this is him—if there is any possibility that it is—I sense a split in my boredom, something other than the whimper of little boys learning to cut a stylus.

Amat has led the visitor into the lecture room and they are standing on the other side of my desk. I look past the top edge of the note and up at the visitor.

He comes into focus before me.

His cloak, made of a fine textured cloth, is pulled tight around his stooped, towering frame. No hair is on the top of his head, but what is left—at the sides and just above his ears—is thick and has grown long and dark-gray over his shoulders. He has no beard, but long eyebrows hang over clear, light-brown eyes. His face, like the rest of him, is long, lean, and full of expression. I have met many men, but this one takes a generous control of the room, lending it the humility of experience, an experience hard-fought.

I can hear the occasional bump against the outside wall. There are faces pushed up against the rough, cloudy glass of the window. Amat has pulled another chair up near my lecture desk. "Please," I say to the visitor, extending my arm toward it.

He sits, his long legs crossed at the knees, his bare calves below his cloak hanging side by side like two great candles. I look toward the sounds at the window and back at him. I am surprised to find him looking only at me.

"Are they always so interested in seeing you?" I ask.

His face creases in a smile. "Only when I choose to be seen."

I look at this man sitting before me and I look at the note he has given me lying on the desk between us.

"Who are you?" I ask.

He allows the question to sit between us, to rest for a moment. He points toward the door. "Who do they say I am?"

There are many who imagine the Created One to be brain sick, grown old and mad, his tale told and retold for so long and for so much listening that he has surely deceived even himself. Some consider him to be the living link back to our very origins, the holder of secrets, a sage, a holy man. Then there are those who think him not a man at all but a being from the stars or the deep of the sea— some other thing that made a woman and then birthed man through her. Perhaps they all have a bit of the truth. For me, as I look into the night stars, I only see that man is too small to know anything of the gods. But for the moment I'll pretend he is who and what his traveling note says he is.

"Surely you know. The masses—they understand so very little yet speak a lot. Where they lack knowledge they make it, they spin it down and excrete it then pass it around to each other like a shared bedpot. Those who have some sense say that you are simply"—I pause—"an old man. A curiosity."

"I suppose that could be said of either of us, yes?" He smiles but he doesn't wait for an answer. "But what do you think, Oren of Susa? Who do you say I am?"

He leans forward in his chair and looks at me.

I feel like I am making a kind of decision, as if I am making some sort of start—forming a beginning with my answer. "I am willing to consider it, to consider that you are the first man."

"That is good. It is important to me, this willingness." He sits back. "Let me tell you a little of it, Oren. Let me tell you what I keep, what I hold onto."

As he begins to speak his eyes grow youthful. A light comes into them, like shadows running from the sun.

"I am an old man. More than nine-hundred and twenty-eight birth years have passed since my waking in Eden. This is true. I am alone as well. My wife, the woman Eve, I saw her one last time before my aide brought me a notice, written by her servitor. Eve had failed to wake several moons past and her burial had been held. I stared at the writing as if it were some riddle. But it wasn't. She was gone."

"You and Eve were not together? You were not with her?" I ask.

"Eve had lived for a long time in a village far to the south. She lived in a home her grandchildren's great-grandchildren built for her. Many of them and their children cared for her in this walled-off house within the village. It had stables, gardens, and fountains as well.

"Word had come before, last midsummer, that she was ill but it took me until the cold season to decide to go and see her. As preparations were made I shooed my servants away from my horse-cart. I chose to ready it for the journey myself. It was a private service, a way of owning the hard work of seeing her again.

"Two full days of travel, we stopped only for individual necessity. My three drivers took turns, one with the reins, one with a spear, and the other at rest. My movements around the country are always known. I think some of my house-servants augment their earnings by selling my plans to the many gawkers and those who imagine me to be something I'm not. Once I would have cared about these whisperings and would have worked to silence them. Instead I've come to you."

I wonder what that could mean, but I decide not to interrupt him.

"Upon reaching the village, it was a spectacle, just as I knew it would be. The marketplace was lined with onlookers, the alleyways clogged with people stopped and pointing as my small caravan proceeded to her house. I sat back, the curtain of my cabin pulled so that I had only a slit through which to look out at them. They all knew who I was. I did not have the same advantage. They were all strangers to me.

"I was led slowly up a turning stairway to her room by a lovely young man. I don't know who he was, and he didn't say his name or ask me mine. He was not rude, just cold, indifferent even, and in no way caught up in who I was. He left me in the hall while he went in and spoke below my hearing before permitting me to enter. He then lingered just out of sight, unwilling to show us any privacy."

Amat is making a record of the meeting. I am sure that as he watches the words he is making, they are unlike anything he's ever imagined writing.

"I came around her bedside and we looked at each other for the first time in a hundred harvests.

"'I insisted they write to you,' she said as my shadow fell across her bed.

"'I am glad you did. You are well cared for.'

"'They are good to me,' she said.

"The outline of her small frame, her thin legs under the linen sheet, was shocking to me. There was so little left of her. Her hair fell over her pillow like seaweed on a rocky beach. I knew that her morning bath had just finished, for the room smelled of bellflower oil and mint.

"As I stood at the side of her bed I had a memory ... a memory from our last year together.

"I had returned from one of my many trips up the edge of the sea. I had been gone for nearly a full season. We had a large pot simmering over the fire and had just added a few seeds and some flakes of one herb or another. As the spices rolled in the broth we both leaned in to smell the steam. Our foreheads touched. Conversation fell silent and we stayed like this for a few brief moments. Frozen in this scene, the cookery a delightful mess, Seth lying on the floor with a kitten he had found; it seemed possible to reclaim ourselves, to become Adam and Eve again. I hesitated to alter the moment with speech but words came. 'It seems perfect to me,' I said. She pulled her head back. 'We need more water,' she said as she turned away without looking at me. I remained there over the pot, the steam forming a layer of dew on my chin.

"Slowly my mind returned to her room and her lying before me all these years later. 'Want some?' She lifted her arm and pointed to a table across the room, on which sat a bowl of fruit. When I turned back she was smiling, the skin of her face pulled from its sag, her eyes brightened but faded back again. I took her hand in mine and kissed it as I bowed and knelt at the side of her bed. I began to cry for the loss of what had once been and out of the regret that I had not held all that we had had more closely. I cried for her beauty and the intimacy we had once had and for a time and place that could never be captured again. I knelt with the deepest wish for even one more day together by the sea. Her hand was soft and cool. I could feel each bone as I pressed it. I saw in her face a failure to make sense of all that we had become. What she saw in my face couldn't have helped. I leaned down and kissed her cheek, which felt against my lips like the loose skin of a dried grape.

"Oren, as I stood to leave, I saw her. I saw what she was and what I was, the first man and the first woman. I saw us and I saw that I now have the language. I can use the words of today to describe what I once saw, the life long past. I now have the words that I need in order to tell the story."

"Your story?" I ask.

"Ours," he says. "I hope it will be ours."

Amat fetches a wine sack. I stand and pour. I hold a goblet out to Adam. He takes it, looks into it and drinks.

"I need to tell it all, not just this part. I need to have it put in words. It is the story of The Maker, of she, and I—The Maker and the made ones."

I sip my wine. This is a bold claim.

"Why me?" I ask. "Why not do it yourself if you have found the language?"

"I have come to you, Oren of Susa. You live it. You see all that man has become. Boys shouldn't grow up to be men who suffer physical distortions and become beggars turned messengers. Orphans shouldn't be orphans, let alone sold in the marketplace like goats. Young men and women engaged in riverside orgies by firelight?"

How would he know of me and her? Surely he is speaking generally of the masses. These things of which he speaks are not unique.

"I was there when all of this was invented, Oren. It is my fault. I own all of this. What man has become is a reflection of who we were. Who I was. I should have done more to protect her. I held it in my hand, this mankind, but I did not care for it. I did not keep, I did not tend. I fell short of the glory for which I was made. And with me fell all this." He holds his arms wide as if to take in the tablet house, Susa, and all that lies beyond.

"And now I am who I am and I have come to you because you can conceive of this and you can help me tell the story. You can help me crack the hull off of it. Pull it clear of the scrub and brush of my memory.

"You are skilled," he says. "Is this not the most respected, the most recognized tablet house in the valley of Susa? You are the teacher of every scribe in employ here and beyond. I am the first man. Together we can tell the story."

I sit silently as he adds to his case.

"Neither you nor I are encumbered with the concerns of family. We are free to do as we wish."

He has inquired about me and has learned a bit. Indeed, this last point is painful for me to hear but is mostly accurate.

I think back to the last time I provided my pen to a man for the purpose of personal writing. It was a boorish, small job. Iashi, the Prince of Uramin, had found me thanks to his now-dead father for whom I had done some court scribbling. Iashi was a young pup, barely off his milkmother's knee and lacking every experience. He wanted to dictate to me his wisdom, the entirety of which he stated to me in less than one afternoon, his rump in his prince's chair, like some self-proclaimed oracle.

As I listen to this man, however, I am taken by the size of the story, the weight of it. Whoever he is, he has come to me when I am ready to take a chance. The sabbatical, the poetry—no, what he is offering is a project of another nature altogether. He has convinced me that he is one who carries a story on his back. True or not, he is asking me to relieve him of it. This is more than writing. His tone and the effort he has made to seek me out—this man holds within him the potential for lasting work.

And if he is who he says he is ... I dare to think of it. His story and my pen—I could trade on his words for the rest of my life. I would be more than a scribe. If this man is who he says he is, I would become like one of the prophets. I would be admitted into the circle of honored holy men. I would be known as Adam's Seer, the one unto whom he chose to divulge the story. And I will have done with it what it deserves.

Adam looks into his drink. "I will come back tomorrow. I will come back the next day. I want it written. I want to tell what happened, make clear the truth of it. Because I know. I know what it was to be in that place and face Him, The Maker. What it was to stand next to Him. I am Adam of Eden."

I am not ready to be pulled into his tale just yet. I will not wait until after the story is told to add weight to my purse. "And what of the payment?" I ask.

"When we are done," he says, "let's discuss it then."

Surely this man knows that no one accepts a job without guarantee. "No," I reply, "now."

"When we are done. When we are done you can have whatever you ask."

I am stopped short by this—an open payment? I am to set my price at whatever I wish?

I stare at him. I think of all he is offering, how his story—even what he's told me so far—so outshines my own poor tale, the slop I've started to write. The boys are trickling in, chattering, taking their seats all around us, and reminding me yet again that I need some time away. The offer of sabbatical—handsomely paid, even—lies here before me.

"Until then, room and board while I work," I say. "And the equal of two season's master scribe payment."

"Whatever you ask. I'll welcome you to my home by the sea for the task."

I should have asked for three seasons, for payment seems to be of no concern to him. I'll be sure to get it at the end.

I look once more at the traveling note resting on my lecture desk. I look up at him sitting there, his wine-purpled lips and gray hair, his eyes peering out at me from under those brows.

"All right," I say. "I will work with you. We will write your story. You will tell it and I will write. You can use my pen, but I'll not promise my silence."

He smiles and folds his hands in his lap. "I woke in the middle of the land of Eden, under a tree. Ripe fruit clustered, dangling stems burdened by the weight. Each leaf fluttered in the sunny evening breeze. Shall we start there?"

Chapter One

Always, Nearly Always

He told me that I sagged as He lifted and peeled me away from the shallow earthen pit, new joints bending for the first time. He had torn away the sod to reveal dark, rich dirt. He had stood in the pit and then knelt, pulling flesh from mud.

The difference between the soil that became me and that which remained behind was in the cup of His hand and the print of His fingers. My flesh bore the run of His thumb where He had closed me up and erased my seams.

With His arm around my shoulders, He pressed His lips against mine. His chest fell as mine rose. His nose rested against my cheek. The Breath filled me.

And I began.

I pulled the warm breeze down my throat. My features, a shadow of His, had been formed and set in their places and now blushed with life.

I was slow to wake. He laid me back into the thick nap of the grass. I released and drew again the fragrant, moist air. A spiraling curl found rhythm and tickled as it fell back and forth, back and forth upon my forehead. I lifted my arm and reached for it. I opened my eyes and saw The Maker.

My first sight. He stood, bent over as if expecting me. I was not sure who He was. But I was sure of Him, a surety like I've never felt since. His appearance brought no concern. He was smiling, so interested in my first movement, most happy to see me. Sunlight dripped and pooled under the shade of the fruiting canopy, rippling across His shoulders and onto my bare torso.

The Maker's hair hung long, coal-black. Brown eyes, deep and shiny, teared as He looked at me. He was youthful, angular, warm and lovely. I don't think I made much expression. I looked around, turning my head only a little. He put His hand to the side of my head, His wrist at my chin. This was a comforting touch, one I knew well.

I looked up into a flush of green, into the tree that had sheltered my birth. Leaves floated in the sun-warmed breeze on the ends of their stems. The leaves seemed to sing, tones and squeaks of delight matching their movement. I wondered if each tree made a different song. It was then that I noticed small winged creatures, their legs like the twigs on which they perched. They hopped in and out of the tree, giving the great plant music.

I looked back at Him.

"The fliers," He said. "They sing and flit in the morning light."

My gaze wandered to the middle of the tree where nests of many shapes and sizes hung at intervals down the trunk. One nest was a deep pocket, another a shallow bowl, and another was hewn out of the skin of the tree itself, its grasses lining a precisely cut hole. Some of the smallest fliers sat on the edges of these nests or a nearby branch, the breeze lifting their down and fluff, forcing them to maintain balance. I considered climbing into the tree among them.

From my spot I studied the great struts, the arms of the tree as they funneled to the center and to the ground. Without joints, the tree was all one piece. One great carving fixed to the grass. Its great base was being scouted by a parade of tiny creatures. Each was like a pair of blackened pebbles stuck together with six legs like black hairs. I watched as each followed the lead of the first, each being the same, a copy. Was this one creature or a group of many?

I must have dozed there in my patch of grass, for I awoke to something soft, warm, and wet, being swept across my hand. I propped myself up on one elbow. The creature lay down against me, curling himself up at my hip. He lifted his chin as I ran my fingers back and forth along the loose skin of his throat. His tail slapped the ground, half-wags beating the grass. I wondered for a moment and, reaching around, I ran my hand down and across my hind-side to my legs. No tail.

In His patience, The Maker had built a fire some steps away. He was cooking.

"I didn't mean for him to wake you," said The Maker. "Are you hungry?"

These sounds from The Maker were so different from those of the beasts around me. What came from Him carried with it not simply song or rhythm, but also meaning.

What came from Him settled not only on my ear, but went further, to the inside of me. Indeed, it sank into me and the thoughts that came in response fell into my throat and bubbled up onto my tongue, my lips released them in phrases that matched His. All of this occurred in moments, faster than I could consider it or make arrangements with myself to conjure for Him an answer.

And so the first words were passed between us.

"Yes," I said. "I am hungry."

The aroma had gathered the words from my lips. The sweet scents of what I would come to know as garlic, honey, and oil—all blending, riding the smoke, tugging at me.

"Good, then let's eat," He said. "The carrots have just the crunch in them that I like so well."

I stood and stepped over to the fireside, my legs under me as if they had been there forever. My head felt light, for the first time so high above the ground. I looked back at my bed. Bits of dry mud, the color of my skin, lay in crumbles and shavings in the grasses that lined the earthen pocket. Still damp, in it I could see my shape. And around my shape His footprints.

I stood with The Maker as He put the last details of our meal in place. He had laid a thin slab of rock across a fire, a rock with a natural bowl in it. Into this He had scooped some water and over this hot water He had steamed the vegetables.

I pointed at some of the food The Maker had prepared.

"Potatoes," He said. Then He pointed at each delight, one after the other. "Radishes, kohlrabi, asparagus, cabbage."

The potatoes were dipped in honey which the fire had encrusted upon them. The radishes, kohlrabi, and asparagus had been rolled in oil and crushed pepper and the carrots were sliced long-ways, still in their peelings. Leaves of cabbage were rolled around "stalks of leek." All of these had come from a kind of woven nest sitting near the fire. As He finished preparations, I picked it up and held it in my hands.

"I call it a basket," He said. "I made the lemongrass and citronella with the idea of a basket in mind."

He took care with each item, giving them a last turn. Then, one-by-one He took them off and sat them on another rock between us. I could see the air rising from them. He then picked up a loaf that was warming at the side of the fire and tore off two pieces.

I watched as He leaned in and took a roll of cabbage and put it in His mouth.

"Try it," He said. "Here, this one."

He handed me asparagus. I held the stalk in front of me and guided it toward my mouth. I felt the warm end of it touch my tongue and I bit down, crunching and chewing. The flavor of it caused me to reach for another even while part of the first one still dangled out of my mouth.

"There you go," He said as He took one of each.

After two handfuls of potatoes I began to slow, looking up at Him now and again, licking the oil and honey from my fingers. He settled back and watched me. He watched me with delight.

"Who are You?" I asked.

"Just as I made the plants with the basket in mind," He said, "I made all you see and touch with you in mind."

"Then you are The Maker," I said.

"Yes, I am The Maker."

"Could I have more ... ?" I searched for the word.

"Bread?"

"... Bread, bread, yes."

And so He gave me a crust of bread and a sip of wine. The wine, which I would learn was being served in half an ostrich shell, sat smooth in the palm of my hand and took on a deep, dark red hue in the growing shadows of afternoon. As we sat, the smoke from the fire curled into the trees, seeming to quiet the calls and chirps. He and I in such shared ease, the evening falling in around us.

"The light," I said.

He smiled. "The sun?"

"Yes, it is moved. The light is going."

"Yes. It will go out. It is the end of the day."

"But it was good. Why must it go out?" I asked. I felt an overwhelming sadness that I'm sure He saw on my face.

He laughed. "It will come back again soon—another day will start."

"Oh." I smiled, relieved. "Good."

"You'll like the night, I hope. I think it is just as wonderful as the day."

"I'm ready."

"I will stay and enjoy it with you."

I woke the next morning in the same spot, in the soft grass under the tree of life. When I sat up I noticed a small creature with long folded hind legs. Its skin glistened as if moist, and its eyes bulged, looking all around. I watched for a moment and then it sprung and landed further away, its padded fingertips holding itself to a stem of palm. I stood to move closer and followed the frog, a name I invented much later.

The creature hopped along in front of me, leading me to the edge of a pool where its hopping became like flight once it entered the water. Seeing the beauty of the pool cut into the rock, I didn't hesitate. I dove in and felt the water pushing against my body, liquid air, cool and soft. I kicked my legs up and down and I moved forward, just as the hopper had done.

With my breath stopped, I went deeper. I could see all around me, to the rock face under the water on all sides. Several creatures came up to me hovering in the water, looking at me with large glossy eyes. They had no arms and no legs and were covered with skin, but shiny and with colors that seemed to change as the light mixed with the water. I reached out to one and ran my hand across its side and over its spiny arches and its flaring tail. It swam in place, moving side-to-side under my touch. Many of these creatures were as long as my own form. I tried to speak to them, but found the water wouldn't allow it. My words came out muffled, trapped in clusters of shiny bubbles, and floated past my face toward the surface.

As I climbed out of the water and onto the rock ledge I looked down and saw my feet. I lifted one into the air before me and stood on the other, like one of the birds I had just come to know. My foot was like a hand built to grasp the soil, pivoting and rolling as I shifted my weight. It had been built for the purpose of treading the land; each toe, the joints working together, hugged the rock on which I stood, lending balance and control.

The Maker was always, nearly always, there.

Together He and I followed valleys and walked their streams until they dumped into rivers. We ventured in and out of dens and deep into caves that He had formed in the rock. In the cool air of these hidden places we lit fires for light. On one visit He made a drawing on the wall of Him and me sitting under a bough of the tree of life.

One afternoon as we walked, I wanted to know more. "This place that You made for me ... how did You put it together?"

The question pleased Him. He smiled and turned to look at me, then moved quickly into the answer—as if He'd simply been waiting for me to ask.

"At first I only thought about it. I imagined how I wanted it to be. I dreamed all of this. Then I announced it aloud to Myself, one wonder at a time. And as I did, there it was, spinning into being all around Me."

"You said it and it was?" I asked.

"Yes ... I suppose that is exactly right," He said, smiling.

I remembered seeing the mud in the grass as I walked for the first time. He must have seen me thinking.

"... All except for you," He said.

"Then how did You make me?"

"I made you with My hands. It took Me the light of an entire day and most of a night."

"Why?"

"I determined to make you different from the plants and animals. I made you like Myself. I made all of you, the parts of you that you can see and those you can't. I molded and carved your body. I fitted each part and sealed you together. Once you were whole, I infused emotion. I cobbled and stamped into your mud form each of your sensibilities and finally your soul."

I was quiet as I listened to The Maker tell me the story of my birth.

"Remember how you like the asparagus better than the kohlrabi?" He asked.

"Yes," I said. "I do like asparagus very much."

He laughed. "Well, I made you to like asparagus. I crafted you in every tiny detail." He came close and put His arm around me. "You are my greatest creation."

I felt what I had felt since my first stirrings, the warmth of being with Him, and an understanding of Him and this place.

I had a desire to create too. I wished to put around and above me a lair or under myself a nest of my own making. I paused on this thought. I could make something new. Ideas of what I might do grew in my mind like the colors of a sunset, filling in, more wondrous as I dwelt and lingered upon them. I came to see this place as it was, a land He intended for me to live in with Him forever. So I made plans to do so.

I had taken an interest in the vegetables, in gathering and planting them so that I could study their growth. One morning I was tending several plants I had brought from near the pool, replanting them in their like groups. As was His way, He would come and watch me. Sometimes, in my focus, I would not notice Him there. He would step forward though, and together we would work. This morning, He asked me for the plants, there were about twelve of them. I handed them to Him and He laid them out for replanting in two lines.

"In this way you can watch them and the harvest basket can sit to the side of each plant," He said, "between the rows."

Rows. I had not thought of such a thing.

In this same way, working beside me, He showed me how to dry figs and apricots by snapping them free and hanging them over their limbs.

"Simply spread their stems and hang them over, some fruit on this side, some on that. They will often fall off when they are dry. So good!"

These dried fruits were indeed a delight to chew while we rode beast-back on the trails I had pruned. He stopped here and there to show off His feats to me.

"Here!" He jumped off His horse, a name I later chose for its power and grace, and hurried to the edge of the trail. "This vine, it is perfect. See the way the stems curl? I clustered the fruit, these orbs with their shiny deep color. They make a sweet, refreshing juice."

He enjoyed a fistful as He held one out to me. "Tell me if you like it."

I rolled the fruit into my mouth and pushed it up between my teeth. As I bit down it popped, spraying the inside of my mouth. I quickly grabbed a cluster.

"I see," He laughed. "Well these are where the wine comes from. I will show you how to make it one day soon."

The juice ran down my chin. I wiped at it, my fingers stained purple.

In this place, this Eden, there was color everywhere. I would not see gray until a great many moons later.

Even the rocks sparkled in their hues and tones. "You colored even these?" I asked as we rode on.

"Colors ran from my fingertips. So I covered the rocks. I thought they, too, should shine with My glory."

We had stopped again, at a waterfall. He stepped into it, the cool water splashing off of Him as He put a hand flat against the smooth cliff. I stood next to Him, the water splashing over me, sparkling in the sunlight.

As we turned up the knoll on the path to my home-place, He held several small, cone-like fruits between His finger and thumb.

"I've seen that one before," I said.

"You have?"

"Yes," I said, laughing. "Why are the seeds on the outside rather than on the inside? It is a fruit that is inside out."

He popped the fruit into His mouth, its leafy green top still attached.

"You can eat it?" I asked. "I did not think that such a strange fruit would be eaten."

"All fruit can be eaten! And this one has nothing in the middle but pure fruit. For this one the seeds were best rolled onto the outside. This way they are rubbed free by each other in the breeze. In working together they make more."

That evening, as we settled in for the night, I asked Him a question that I'd had for some time.

"Why do some of the lights in the heaven shine bright and others dim?"

He turned His face up at the night sky, as if studying it with me.

"It is not flat up there like a leaf. It is deep and wide like a great upturned empty pool. Some of these lights are placed at the far reaches of the pool, others are close. The spaces between them are greater journeys than any to be taken anywhere."

I searched for words. "So they float in the empty pool, these lights, as a show? Or do they serve some purpose?"

"They are there as a touch of light, a note that I was there, and to them I have lent a bit of My glory so that they coat the night sky for you. It is so that you'll never be in darkness."

That was it, one evening in thousands with Him; the two of us standing together, our shoulders touching in this place He had once only imagined, our noses pointing toward the dark and the glitter.

And I did not know to consider that such wonders as this night were mine to lose. Pleasures like fresh-cut rye once gathered in armloads. All past now. Burnt, like chaff.

Oren of Susa: Concubines in Pairs, Walking

I am back in my room at the far end of Adam's house. Here sits my cloak and case, exactly where I left them this morning before eating two oranges, drinking some tea, and being rushed off by the votary to meet with Adam. I toss the dry orange peels out the window and then sit at the edge of the bed and unstrap my boots. My eyes blur with fatigue. My neck is as stiff as a sheepman's staff and my right hand and wrist ache as if they've been tied in a knot all day.

With my bare feet on the cool stone floor I think about how this man walked into my tablet house, the crowd straining to get a glimpse of him, and how he filled the chair across from my lecture desk with mystery, how he stole my imagination and talked me into leaving my teaching and coming here to his house to live and to listen. I am about to spend weeks—months, a year?—recording his story. And after a full day of work I am no closer to having my questions answered than I was then. He told me he was Adam and now he's telling me his story. Even as we start it I still wonder if this man can possibly be who he claims to be. He has hired me, so this story is mine to write. But alongside that, this story is mine to believe.

Or not believe.

What I do know is that it feels good not to be surrounded by a pack of boys when indoors and the mass of illiterates when out.

The young servant who has been assigned to me knocks at my door and then announces himself by calling out his name—Mahesh or Mavish, something like that— several times in rapid succession until I reach the door and open it. He stands there looking pleased, holding a tray on which sits my supper—a whole roasted duck on a bed of cranberries, a bowl of potatoes with dill, and a large wooden tumbler of beer.

"Is there anything else I can gather for you, Scribe Oren?"

The servant could not be more cheerful. This grates on me. But rather than taking my tray from him and sending him on his way, I stand back, let him fully into my room and close the door behind him. He sets the tray down on a small table by the window and turns to face me. He stares at the door, his mouth half open in confusion.

I speak before he can. "Tell me about Adam."

The servant looks at me, surprised. "My master, Scribe Oren?"

"Yes, yes. Tell me about him. Tell me about Adam."

The servant looks around the room as he gathers his apron and wipes his hands. "He is a kind man, this is certainly true. He provides everything we need. My family and I have made a home here on this land. He's generous, quiet, and strong."

This is not what I am looking for, well-rehearsed praise tells me nothing. "We're behind a closed door," I say. "Talk to me about Adam, will you?"

The servant looks anxious. I assure him that nothing he says will get back to Adam. I say that I just want his insight. I ask more directly, I ask about Adam—the man— where he came from and what his servants think of him.

His eyes brighten as if he's finally understood what I'm asking. He stands up a bit straighter as if he will now enlighten me. "There is no secret," he says. "My master is the first man of creation, of course!"

Of course.

I turn and open the door. "Thank you for supper," I say.

"Is there anything else?" asks the servant as he moves into the hall. "Anything at all?"

I dismiss him with a comfortable lie. "You've been most helpful, thank you," and I shut the door.

I pull a stool over to the table under the window and as I begin to eat I look at the writing I've completed. These are Adam's words. They have been hard earned.

It was easier with that young prince of Uramin so many years ago. He had droned on all day delivering thoroughly cropped and procured statements. He was a fool, but he knew how to speak. I'd simply sat in silence and written it all down.

But Adam has been like a child telling of his first hunt, the details spilled out in excited fragments and half-thoughts. Important moments were run past to get to the next thought, then circled back upon and retold to give a missing or meaningless detail. I kept stopping him. "Adam, Adam, please. Slow down. What did The Maker say as He made your evening meal? Something about a crutch?" Adam paused, his hand dropping mid-gesture into his lap. "No, crunch, the carrots crunched and He said He liked them that way." And he was off again. "Wait, Adam. Hover. Stay in these moments and let's walk around them a couple of times." He had been so eloquent when we'd met, yet I found that I had to teach him to tell his story.

As a result of this effort and the constant crashing of the sea, I suffered a noise of the mind, anxiety at the job. The writing straw stood too tight in my fist. At times my mind took over and Adam became part of a long conversation I was having with myself. His bits of reporting expanded on the page as I grabbed details that he had given me out of order, or in asides, added clarifications that I asked for because they seemed to be missing, and tried, as we stumbled along, to balance and make order of the mess piling up between us.

And there was that old dog—pure gray, gaunt, its fur in greasy knots, lying at Adam's feet all day. As Adam told me of his dog in Eden I looked down at this dog. Was it breathing? As if sensing my stare, it opened its eyes and looked at me. Eyes like marbles set in mud looked straight at me and then vanished again behind curtains of wrinkled hairy eyelid. Was this that same dog? "Oren, are you listening?" asked Adam.

I had stopped writing. As if woken from a sleepwalk, I caught myself. "Yes, I am listening, sorry, yes—please continue."

Adam looked at me as if to ask if I was alright but then began again, quickly getting back up to speed. I rubbed the back of my neck and focused again on the movement of my stylus.

Adam asked me midmorning if he could read what I wrote, if he could look it over at the end of each day or every couple of days and fill in gaps with a bit more of the "sense of it all." I told him this would be fine. I said this mostly to satisfy him so we could move on. I know when the time comes and he reviews the story he will not be filling in anything. He will simply be amazed at the artful job I will have done in giving his story form and order, of putting the details where they belong.

Every other hour or so we stopped working and rested for a few moments. There was usually some servant or visitor Adam had to speak with—answering questions, giving direction. All daily business—marketplace news, crop planning. At every one of these breaks I spent the time rubbing my wrist, resting my eyes, and considering whether or not to pack up and leave. I wondered at his jumbled telling of the story. He had told others, he had surely told them something? But then we'd start again and with each part of the story, this man seduced me with his clumsy passion for this tale.

So, sitting here alone in my room at the end of this first day of work, my mouth full of duck and beer, I am committed. Hard work though it is, this story would be impossible for me to turn my back upon. I know myself, and if I left I would revisit the decision a million times. No one else has such a story. The possibility of who this man could actually be—that is what is going to keep me here.

Mankind has become so sure of itself, so confident in its own prowess. Tales like this one are easily dismissed. The purveyors of talk like Adam's are too often worshiped as gods or considered delusional. But this man seems to be neither of these. He is confident and the details he gives are rich. He seems to know of what he speaks—albeit with an unwieldy passion. He carries authority.

He told me today of the safety and happiness he felt with this person—this Maker and Father, this Teacher with whom he'd sat and spoke and traveled Eden. As I listened to him I thought of my own father. My maker. He taught me too—stood over me for hours on end as I wrote the letters and the numbers, telling me I was not fit to cut the stylus of the dullest boy in the class and demanding that I try again until I wept. What Adam told me is so different. The telling of it feels like an elaborate dream he's had and has now come to claim as personal history. It could also be the origins of mankind. And for this I secretly hope. I want Adam's story to be true because it is so—wonderful.

I see that I am circling, pacing the perimeter of this room over and over. I need to clear my head, to go for a walk.

The sun is setting as I step outside. Adam's home is a stretch of several buildings spaced out facing the sea. They are long structures, one level only, crafted of wood, stone, and earth. They are covered by thick grass roofs, woven into place and lashed tight. The buildings are connected by paths covered by trellises and vines. The place is very well kept, plants are trimmed, and paths are raked. Fruiting trees in large pots cast shade over the yards between the buildings. To one side of the compound are rocky pastures with clumps of long grass where livestock graze between small homes and farm buildings. To the other side is the sea, the shoreline with its sand and rock stretching in either direction. Seabirds circle in the light of day's end, landing and retreating up the beach from the lapping surf.

The paths are lit with lamps and the breeze has settled. As I walk I see several pairs of women, concubines I assume, walking the paths as well. A man like this, with such a story and such a place must surely have women who serve his every need. They stop whispering to each other and make eye contact with me each time I pass them. Each of them is wearing a different colored outer wrap and loose-fitting scarf.

As I am about to pass one pair for the second time they stop short and turn toward me. They are neither young nor old. Their skin is colored with some plant or another and their eyes shine from under closely trimmed brows. They wear spikes of polished ivory in their ear lobes. I stop, too, and stand looking at them, not sure what is expected of me. Then one of them speaks.

"Do you want to know what he is like when no one is here?"

The way they ask me this, I know that they know who I am and why I am here. But I'm surprised by this. I am a stranger. There is no reason they should approach me.

Even so the women rightly take my pause as a desire to hear the answer.

"He has a habit of going out every seven days and standing upon the highest point on the beach and calling out to the clouds, singing to The Maker."

I'd like to talk to this Maker. I'd like to get some answers about all of this. Perhaps I'll join him at this.

"Does The Maker meet him there?"

"No," said the other, "The Maker doesn't come."

"Can he see The Maker, perhaps see him listening from far off or see him pass by?"

"No, The Maker isn't visible, but he says he can see Him. Adam says he can see The Maker just as a blind man can see his lover enter the room."

"And what do you think of this?" I ask the women.

"I find the mystery of it to be wonderful," says one.

"Yes, me too," says the other. They are speaking more to each other than to me. "He is unlike any other man."

The women seem at ease with the thing as they gaze past me, over my shoulder. I turn and look out to sea. The sun is in its last moments, pooling light onto the surface of the water.

Above the sun hangs a single cloud—like a curl on a forehead.

Chapter Two

Mesh of Wood and Leaf

One afternoon, our bellies full of food and wine, He suggested we set out on one of our common walks. He knelt on one knee at the edge of the fire. The bottom of His drinking pot formed a ring in the dirt as He picked up the last few lima beans between His fingertips and thumb. I was sitting back, my legs crossed at the ankles. The bottoms of my feet, stretched out toward the fire, had grown soft and warm.

"This last drink makes me want to ride," I said lazily.

"No. I must show you a less simple place, you and me alone. The sooner we get there, the sooner we can return."

It was an odd decree that we travel on foot. His mood pivoted on the matter.

"What is the harm in riding?"

He did not respond.

I leaned another log into the flames. Sparks sailed up toward the treetops and I settled back again. "If we are going to travel on foot then let's wait until morning when we have rest and a full day of light ahead of us." I gave Him a moment then continued. "We will rise early and leave. We can have our morning meal along the way."

He stood and pitched his remaining wine into the fire. The flames hissed.

"Let's go."

My four-legged one rose from his slumber at my elbow, stretched, and trotted down the edge of the nut orchard, turning and melting into the lengthening afternoon shadows.

"A few moments then," I began to pull my legs under me. "I'll gather my traveling sack ... there are a few things I like to take when we—"

"No. You won't need anything. Let's go."

As He turned away the fire died down and my newly added log rolled off to one side, smoking but not burnt.

As we left I called for my tailed companion. He did not come.

Within minutes, leaving a familiar path, we slipped into the undergrowth and began a slow, steep, side-winding descent. Once in the valley, catching one of our eastern-most trails, we set off in the direction of a stand of the noblest trees. Such trees stood out in contrast to the rest in Eden and against the darkening evening sky.

My legs tingled. The ground, cool and damp, was uneven under my feet. I rocked with each step, tottering. At first I had felt a certain joy in the use of my body, at spending my energy and exerting myself. I demanded more of myself the further we went, and for a great distance I found no limits. But in time all I could think of was my aching, tired body. It had been hours since we'd last paused to sit. I imagined a chip of slate sunk into my lower back, another slid in and wedged under my right shoulder bone. "Why such a rush? Why the demand in our pace?" Between my panting and shuffling I had muttered too low for Him to hear. He was like a gust at my back, chasing me, forcing a hurried nearly desperate gait.

The moon stood full and bright, bathing us in soft white light as we hustled along. My shoulders slumped and my knees took on a constant bend as if I carried a burden. My mouth hung in an oval as breath rushed in and out of me. I lifted my wrist and wiped the sweat from my forehead in an effort to stop the stinging in my eyes. This walk had become hard work. A march. We were going further than we had ever gone.

I dropped to the inside at a bend in the trail. The softer soil at the edge and the moss that grew there made my steps easier. The fuzz gave a bit under each foot, cradling my beaten heels. My open palm pushed off each tree as we went. I heard His solid, even steps close behind me until He finally eased around me, two steps to my left, and He was leading.

I fell back and began to doze as I walked. I took more steps with my eyes closed than open. I perceived that my companion was behind me, panting, his feet falling hard, in rhythm, a trick of the hour and my weakness. Carrying myself along, I started to turn as if to give him a rub on the chin and help him along.

"Come there ... here's a scratch for you ... lift your tail, thirsty one."

At that moment, my hand dangling toward the empty trail at my heels, a leafy branch slid across my ear and down the back of my neck. I sprung to one side, jerked fully awake. Arms flailing, my hands swatted at empty air. I started into a panicked run.

I assumed The Maker was up ahead of me. I could no longer see Him or hear anything but my own excited breathing and the thump of my heart. I turned another bend and sped up as the path swept wide around an outcrop of rock. The trees thinned in spindly arches as I sped beneath them. As I came around and the path straightened out, there He was. Had His pace slowed? No, He had stopped! I twisted sideways, hopping, sliding on loose dirt. I narrowly avoided running headlong into or over Him.

I stood beside Him, my hands on my knees. "I'm tired."

"I know you are."

He looked up the trail and then into the sky without looking at me.

"I'm hungry," I added anyway, following His gaze.

The rising sun turned the heavens toward a cool, cloudless indigo blue. Most of the stars had lingered to welcome these first hints of dawn. A light breeze kicked up to help push the night along. The Maker looked over at me as I stared up, as if suggesting I should be concerned with something else. I was. My feet felt as if they were twice their size and on a bed of hot coals. I started to sit down but He began to move again at a slow, focused pace. I stayed on my feet, heartened by His leisurely cadence. He seemed not to be listening or watching, but sensing, turning His head, lifting his hands and feeling the air, not using the trickling dawn, yet seeing much.

We skirted a small pool and descended only a few steps before crossing a thin stream, water just over our knees, a crevice in the forest. With the first step the water lifted my mood, salve to my feet and ankles. My backside dipped into it and I touched the cool flow. As I cupped my hand to my mouth, I heard the familiar slapping of rock, a waterfall somewhere nearby. I wanted to go lie down in it.

As we passed over the next rise the water ran down my legs, and with the breeze caused a shiver. He slowed a bit more as I followed. The birds' dawn singing faded behind us. We stepped off the path. The forest opened up and flattened out and the morning light faltered. For there stood a tree, one great specimen above and beyond all others, its great mass having long ago starved those in its shadow. He stopped, standing, just beyond its reach. I stepped around Him, pushing aside my aches and wants.

Great boughs hung over me, as I think of it now, like the skewed beams of a shipwreck. Any advancing light was dimmed under the twisted mesh of wood and leaf suspended over me. I could not see the top of the tree from under it, and I had failed to take note of its height as we approached. At my feet, popping up here and there from the earth, were roots, arched and without bark. The half-loops they formed threatened to trip me. I was forced to look down.

The air grew cooler as I moved inward, step by step toward its base. There I met a trunk unlike any I had ever seen, a great curved wall of bark, like cobblestones set in iron. I leaned in and stepped up onto its base where it sloped up from the ground. The trunk felt like a reptile's back, alive yet unfeeling, returning no warmth.

I started to speak, to ask questions and understand His purpose with this creation, this tree in the eastern reach of Eden. But I realized that He had not followed me in under the tree. He had stayed outside its canopy. I had run ahead. I was alone in the shadow of this great hull.

Stepping down from the trunk's base I turned and looked back. He showed no sign of joining me in my discovery. He stood still, eyes closed. The wash of blue dawn made Him stand out against the flowering and fruited bramble.

I remembered the tree under which I had been born. The life that lived around and within its boughs was constantly changing, flourishing. This tree I now stood under did not allow any such sharing of space. The leaves were like large green skins spread thin between spindling bones. Deep creases made them appear to be stretched and sewn.

Looking closer I noticed that one of the fruits of the tree dangled within reach. As I moved toward the fruit, and deeper under the yawning canopy, the place was more cave-like. Many of the great branches hung heavy and low toward the ground. I approached the fruit and using both hands I grasped the ivory-colored orb. It held tight to its ropey stem as I used my weight to break it free.

Dense and heavy, the outer finish was like that of a citrus. The rind had deep dimples which my fingers slipped easily into, as if the fruit had been formed, squeezed into shape and hung. My forefinger arched like a sickle, I scratched the rind and held the large bulb to my nose. The scent was full and crisp; it spread inside me, filling my chest. I dug in with my thumb and pulled another deep, delicious breath. My nostrils went wide as the cool air rushed across the juicy gash, numbing my senses. My head went light and my balance faltered. I felt a touch at my side. My breathing stopped shallow, the skin on my skull and neck went tight. He had placed His hand at my back just under my ribs. I exhaled. The fruit still palmed tight in my hands.

He stepped around me and looked at the juice running down my arm. He then looked at me, the inner circle of His eyes wide in the shade.

"I don't think I've seen one before." I tried to appear calm, relaxed.

"This tree is the only one of its kind," He said. "It is alone."

The juice began to drip from my elbow. He held a finger under to catch a drop and rubbed the tacky nectar between His fingers.

"It surely smells ... good." I used the word I had heard Him use to describe all He had made. As I held it out to Him He pulled away so I lifted it back to my nose.

Just as I started to inhale a third time, He put His hand over the fruit and pushed my arm down to my side.

"Yes, it is good, but once it is on the tongue, all is made known."

He wrenched the fruit from my hand and tossed it back toward the far side of the tree. It bounced with a thud and spun to a stop, its rind laid open, deep-pink pulp exposed and bleeding. I stared after it. The dirt under it grew dark and muddy.

"I must tell you," He continued, "all is not good. There is more that tasting this fruit will bring; there is more that you don't know."

"More of this land, this home you have made for me?"

"No. More that is not good. I've called it evil. I have hemmed in the evil to keep it away, and this tree is its gate."

I motioned to the luster all around us. "If it is not like all of this I can't imagine it."

"It is good that you cannot imagine what is not good," He said.

This made sense to me but it fed my curiosity. There was something other than all that I knew, something other than good? I looked back at the fruit. I remembered how I had felt moments before, alone under the tree while He stood back. Was this the cool shade of evil?

For the first time He looked up into the tree. No branch was straight; no branch was like the next. "It is not simple," He said, "giving form to such a thing. My original idea has certainly grown and taken shape."

"I would like to know more," I said. Nervousness and curiosity rattled in my head. "I would like to know more ... of this."

"I know you would," He said, still looking up. "But this tree is not a beginning, it is an end. To taste of it is to leave all else behind. To taste of it is to die in its shadow."

"Die?"

"Life can be taken away, slowly replaced with dry stillness. Dust without breath."

"This knowledge brings a death? To taste of it is to know and die?"

He took a step toward me. "I have given you all things, everything you see and will ever see. And I now give you this tree. But I give it to you so that you may leave it alone." He spoke slowly, intentionally, choosing His words. "You can have all else. It is yours. But I brought you here, to this tree, to warn you and ask you to leave it as it is."

"To show me ... you brought me all this way to show me what I cannot have?"

He looked at me, studying my face. He smiled. "I'll keep nothing from you. All I have is yours. I brought you here to show you this, to show you what you should not have." He turned and started back toward the trail.

"You must have knowledge of this evil," I called out after Him. "What is it like?"

He stopped walking and looked at me, over His shoulder, without turning back. "You felt the bark of the tree didn't you?"

I nodded.

"This is its soft side," He said.

He continued on to the trail. I did not follow and He did not wait.

Once more I looked at the drying pulp in the mud. I rubbed my nose. The scent was trapped in the tiny folds of the skin of my knuckles.

Full sunshine now bathed the trail. I could see the top of the tree from there. It hovered against the sky like a deep, leafy mountain. I turned and descended, beginning the long walk back home. I stepped into the stream again. Slowly I washed my hands as I crossed. Rubbing the water between my fingers and rinsing, I repeated His words aloud to myself.

"Leave it as it is."

A creamy, yellow dampness hung in the air as I came back across my fields, toward the house. The man who had traveled only a day and a night before was now so naïve, so young. Under that tree He had told me things, things I did not care to know.

I collapsed into my bed rack. My pet curled at my feet.

"Leave it as it is. Leave it as it is."

Oren of Susa: What I Saw

My servant's name is Mahesh. I've finally settled that. I saw his name written in a list of house servants on the wall near Adam's quarters.

Each of the servants is taught to write their own name for the purpose of being able to give notice of their attendance. Other than that, they appear to have no writing or reading skills. I've left all the writing I've done so far— Adam's story up to this point—lying on the table in my room, in an open crate. The sheets of vellum are stacked. A sheet of slate lies on top to keep them from curling. It is clear as Mahesh straightens my room each day that he's not gotten into it. The crate sits in the same spot, at the very angle I left it. It is an odd thing to me to think that none of the house staff will read Adam's story. Perhaps it will be read and told to them. This is how stories are shared among them. There is a gathering on the beach every few days and stories are told from memory or more recent happenings are told as recreation and as news. I've listened in on these sessions a few times and they are very good storytellers. I've heard the story of a huge fish that washed up onto the shore and about how the sun was once covered up at midday—even as it was shining bright—and how it stayed that way for some time. The older of us in the crowd have seen such events, but the younger ones and children laughed in disbelief.

Adam and I are finished for the day and it is earlier than usual—too soon for our evening meal. I am surprised to find that I have some energy left in me. I don't feel worn thin and made empty from the work of writing as is so often the case by the time we stop late in the day. I can feel the stress of operating the tablet house beginning to lift from my back. I think I'd like a longer walk, perhaps to a village. I need some time and space to let settle all I've heard.

Mahesh tells me there is a village nearby. He says I can't see or hear it from here, but it is close enough I can walk there and back by nightfall. He scrapes a crude map of lines and arrows onto the inside of a piece of bark and hands it to me.

After listening to Adam, the trees look different to me as I walk under them on the road into the village. I walk slowly and study them. The air is cool in their shade and the oldest ones have knots and knobs up and down their trunks. Limbs hang over me like the bony fingers of an ancient giant.

Adam told me of the beginning of evil, or how he discovered its existence. As I think about it I realize someone had to be first. Not just to live as he did in Eden, but to also meet this darkness and its potential. Adam's telling sits with me as if having revealed a fact. On the road to the village this afternoon I have seen a blind child sitting naked in the door of a shack. Thin arms and legs, upturned face, gray milky eyes roll side to side as he listens to my passing footsteps. I've also seen an old man riddled with sores, scraping himself with a shard of pottery as he sits by a fire while his friends lecture him on his morals.

I enter the village through the wooden gate and walk down the main cart path. I am welcomed with slight nods. Some give me a formal greeting: "The day's sun warm you and the breeze rest at your back." And others give a simple hello. The place has all the sense of daily life— woodsmoke hangs in the air, a handful of she-goats are being led to their milking by a pair of boys, a team of oxen stand unyoked, drinking from a trough as a farmer sits and dozes on a short stool next to them.

I walk past low-slung dwellings with slanted roofs and larger homes with coned grass tops. Tucked between and around these are stone-fenced plots where chickens are pecking or gardens are set. Leaving the path and weaving between these dwellings, I find the day market. I begin to sort through the goods on the first table—small bags made of hide. I lift one to look at it and I notice, past it and across the street, just as we have in Susa, there is a small house with the symbol on the side of it. It is a house where women and girls are fed well and clothed richly, then rented to men by day or night.

I don't know much of these places. I've certainly never been to one. It is a filthy business that they do, and I've always tried to ignore them. But I notice a conversation happening at the side of the road in the front of the house. Two women—one younger and the other older—are talking with a man. I watch as the older woman shakes her head and holds up several fingers. The man reaches under his cloak and hands her a small sack of coins. He puts a leather strap around the younger woman's wrist and leads her away. The younger woman looks back over her shoulder at the older woman as she is taken down one of the paths between the buildings and is gone. The older woman pulls open the drawstring of the sack and peers inside.

I am standing at the edge of the market. I am made uncomfortable by what I've just seen and it is obvious that I was watching. Staring. The older woman looks up and sees me. Before I can retreat back into the market, she is coming over to me.

I'm not sure what to say. "I am not interested in ... I was only standing here—"

She interrupts. "You are the one writing Adam's story," she says.

It takes me a moment to realize the woman is not approaching me for business. I remember Adam mentioning to me that some of his servants tell what they know of his comings and goings in exchange for goods or money. I wonder if I am now somehow part of that trade. I don't answer the woman quickly enough.

"What has he told you?" she asks. "What sort of things are you hearing?"

I hesitate. I enjoy my privacy and I know Adam does too. "He's telling me about his early life and how he learned that all is not good." I leave out any mention of The Maker or of Eden.

She looks down at the sack she's clutching. "He learned that all is not good," she repeats.

"That is what he has told me," I say.

Her hair is cared for and held up with thin golden pins. Her face is washed and powdered. I grant that all this effort is perhaps hiding her age but it is not hiding her worry or her anger. Her eyes are red all along the inside edges. "That was my youngest daughter I just gave to that man for the night. He gave me enough money to buy both of us food for a week."

I wish I had not stepped into this scene and that I could slip away. I wish I'd stayed in my room, drank some tea or taken a nap.

"By nightfall I'll be with a man too, and I'll earn not half of what she has earned and she and I will meet in the morning and we will live for another day. We will cry and we will sleep in the shade. We will wash the smell of the men from our necks and breasts. And maybe we'll take one night to rest. But we'll not take two."

"I'm sorry," I say.

"He learned that all is not good? I have children by a dozen men and grandchildren by a half-dozen more."

I look up at the house so that I don't have to look at her. I feel ashamed for what other men have done, but I have no idea what to say to such things.

"Tell him," she says, "tell Adam if he'll hear it. Tell him all is not good. Tell him it never has been."

The woman turns and walks toward the house. She crosses the street away from me and doesn't look back. One of the men reclining in the front watches her go in and enters the house behind her.

I turn back and face the marketplace. The stalls with their tables of goods have lost their interest for me. I walk back through the village, past the sights and sounds of simple life, under the trees and into the pastures toward Adam's house, toward the sea.

It is getting late when I return. The sun is bright, but low on the horizon. Adam is at the water's edge cleaning a pair of fish he's netted. I stand and watch as he works.

"Do you get much fresh fish in Susa?" he asks.

I don't know what to say. I can only think of that woman and her daughter.

"A little, yes." I pause then start. "The evil that you spoke of, under the tree ..."

"Yes, Oren?"

"I was in the village this afternoon. I saw it all around me."

Adam doesn't look up. "I know."

"I've always thought," I say, "that the poor and lame are the way they are because that is the way of life. It happens just as a tree grows crooked in the forest or doesn't fruit. Normal is sometimes made different by fate."

"I wish it were so simple, so easy to set aside."

"But you've told me of the tree, the origin of all this suffering."

"I have, yes."

In the sharp light of the sunset I see the past carved in the skin of Adam's face. He bears down on the knife. I hear the spine of the fish splinter. I know that he will tell me. In the days to come he will tell me that he did not leave evil as it was.

"How do you live with it?" I ask. "How do you live with this knowledge of the beginning? Of how life once was?"

"I carry it. I hold it like lava that once flowed in and filled my chest and has hardened into jagged rock."

And I see. The man has grown old under the weight of this regret—perhaps because of it. I have regrets too. He and I are alike in this, but my regrets are only for me. They are only mine.

"When you tell me about it—maybe by my writing it—you will find some relief."

"Yes, that is my hope. I have told The Maker of my sorrow, of my empty wishes that I had done differently. I have told Him over and over. And now I will tell you. And then I'll be done telling it."

I wonder to myself where Eve is in all of this. She has not yet come into the story. I hope when she does, he tells her about the tree—that he protects her from it.

Chapter Three

At the Soles of My Feet

For many seasons after, I could not look at any fruit without thinking about that one under that tree. I now had the idea that this place and all I had been born into was not a certainty. It could be lost. This truth hung like a new smell in the air as I continued to create my home with its gardens and orchards.

Even so, my daily contentment was complete. I was delighted with this place and my abilities to rule over it. There was nothing it needed that I couldn't muster. I went to bed ready for rest and I woke with the energy for another day.

I learned to count time. At first I noticed the frequency of the watering that came to the ground. I made a scar-tree, forming a stroke in the bark for each rising mist. But soon I saw a pair, a match in the coming and going of the mists and the shape of the moon. I saw in the gaps of their arrival a rhythm, a pattern which told me when each plant would give me its goods. In this way I determined the season of the fruiting of certain plants, such as the barley and other common seeds. This simple counting of time became important to me. I saw and made note of the span, the life lived between my awakening and the now.

So it was in this way that I knew I had been at work for four moons and half of another one, hoisting the stones now scattered about into an archway over the entry to my homeward path, the bases on either side wide and tall enough for a horse and rider.

I nibbled from a small pouch of nuts and grain. I had made the pouch by a craft of folding large leaves in layers upon each other and leaving them to dry in the sun. I nibbled as I wandered slowly from stone to stone, seeking just the right edge, just the right shape. I turned to realize The Maker was sitting on one of the larger stones watching me. I noticed Him there just as I was inspecting the next stone I needed and realized it was serving as His footstool.

"I could offer you another," I said as I sat down next to Him.

I tossed a bit of the mixture I was eating toward a small huddle of what I would come to know as juncos.

"They'll eat as much as I give them," I continued.

He stood and rolled the rock several times toward the base of the arch. "It's the flying. It makes eaters of them."

"Wings and beaks go together," I thought out loud. "Flapping and pecking."

I hung the pouch from a nearby branch and stepped over to the rock The Maker had rolled toward the arch.

"I've been thinking," He said. "I have made all of this

and now you are my heir. I would like to involve you more in it somehow."

I stopped to listen. I knew the tone and that I needed to pay attention. An idea was coming, fast.

"What can I add? These creatures, this place, neither are lacking in any way."

"I want you to name them," He said. "Name them all. This is a task you can do, I am sure of it."

His suggestion seemed odd to me. Name them? What was wrong with "the animals" or "those creatures", or "that one"? I looked down at the birds I was feeding. Name them? Why? I had not said it aloud, but still He answered.

"It will be a way of providing for them as your own."

I stared at Him. "But they are scattered," I said, gesturing with a wide sweep in every direction. "They are moving all the time. How will I label them?"

"You will go to them, and they will come to you. You will look at them, study them, and pronounce their names."

I felt a flush of panic. "All of them? This is more than I can do. I don't have the first idea. I lack your understanding of these creatures. How would I do such a great task?"

"I will offer you the help of an angel. One who has the skills you need. This angel will meet you before your first night's camp."

"An angel?"

"A creature of my making, not bound to this place like the others. And not a man, like you, but rather a creature made to serve."

"Do you have a special command I can pronounce to bring the animals to me?" I was spinning, searching, hoping that some concern of mine might slow the conversation down and bring reason.

"The best suggestion I have is to start," He said.

I lifted the stone, hoisting it up to my waist and setting it on the rising stack to the other side of the path. It balanced perfectly, the edge and heft of the rocks joining as if one.

The next morning, after sleeping restlessly and much later than was my habit, I packed a few items for the journey. As I did so, I paused, surrounded by all that had once been so new to me. All that still delighted me. I looked around at this place I was leaving; this very spot was where I had lived since my first day.

Over time, like the creatures around me, I had given over to my impulse to build, to create. I had built a home, covering it on all sides with braided leaves and vines, and later with river-mud I had formed walls and then a grass roof. This was my warren, this small clearing, these structures. I had built also the winepress and fruit shed. I had cleared all the spots where I'd planted gardens, thick with vegetables or flowers, various types side by side. Bringing them from near and far, I had put them under my watchful eye to study. I had gathered into my orchard over seventy and five different fruiting trees.

I didn't know how long I'd be gone, and when that is the case it is hard to leave.

In my bag I packed some flint for making fires or for cutting, several blank tablets, reeds, and some rope; whatever I had imagined might help me get the job done. I also carried a drawing I had made of the lands around my home. Within the first day's walk I began to add details to the drawing, pushing the lines, winding them well on beyond anything I had known.

I traveled deep into the land that first day. Had I not been looking for the angel, I may have moved past without taking notice of it. The angel was not looking for me and the evening shadows were growing long and heavy. I spotted the creature, or what I assumed it was, eating from among a spread of berries. It was fit and graceful in its movements, shaped like a man but smooth, hairless, with a solid and still color, like dried milk. It turned and saw me and lifted an arm to eat another handful of berries. Even as I stopped and stared, it made no expression. When it finally turned to me I was drawn to its only color, thin lips and tapered fingertips stained a deep blue-purple. It approached me confidently. I stepped back out of its path, seeing that it knew its way, and began to follow.

As the day neared an end we had traveled some distance. The angel simply paused and stood still. Was it listening for animals or watching and studying their marks in the soil? It held still as I came close. I was about to ask when it spoke.

"We must stop here. This is a spot they like." The angel had its own way of speech, very smooth, each sound hung in order. It was as if the angel had just learned my language.

"How do you know this?" I asked.

The angel looked past me, never at me. "There is water. There is cover."

I was partly impressed. The angel knew the land and had made acquaintance with the animals or had been told in great detail of their habits. It had put itself to the task.

It was the angel that suggested we travel about and name the animals as we saw them. But I was not impressed with its silence. The creature lacked, or had set aside, any personality.

Late that night after we made our sleeping burrows, I found myself staring into the fire for a long time. Conversation had become like sunlight to me. It had been little more than a full day since I had talked with The Maker. Only a few hours had ever gone by without our speaking to one another. The last talk with Him had been so formal. He had looked at me, into my eyes, and made His demand. Even so, I wanted to hear His voice. I listened, craving some sound from Him. I was still listening as sleep fell over me.

I lay still in the predawn darkness as the first morning calls of animals surrounded me. Was it many more than usual? I could hear the rustling of grasses, the snap of branches and crunch of leaves with their movements. But what was that something else I was hearing? The breeze, yes, but under it ... under it was a rumble, a push, as if the very forest were sliding in on itself, coming toward us under the clear, dawning sky. I got up on my knees and then my feet and listened again. I could feel it in the earth at the soles of my feet. I stepped out toward the clearing and stood next to the smoldering ash of last night's fire.

Before me was an immense gathering: the greatest throng of creatures I'd ever seen and would ever see again.

The trees around the clearing were loaded with all kinds; small animals hanging by their tails, perched, and sitting up on branches clutching seeds or nuts in their front paws, others lying back in the crotches of the branches. Some of the limbs bowed, nearly touching the ground. I wondered if the trees might collapse and splinter under the weight of them.

The sky above me swirled with birds. Small ones hummed as they floated down and settled in the bushes, others as tall as me settled into the tree tops flapping, their wings cracking against the air.

And covering the clearing as it rolled away from us in every direction as far as I could see stood the beasts of the ground. The breath of the creatures rose like smoke into the first strands of morning sunlight. Calls and bellows sounded all around us, echoing into and out of the forest. Heads lifted back, snouts and muzzles pointed toward the clear sky. Hooves and paws had pounded the grasses and smaller plants into pulp. The farthest distance moved in shifts of color and texture, while the scene nearest me was filled with the smallest creatures scurrying back and forth, stopping, tails held high, ears up and listening.

I lifted my hands to my head in wonder. And as I did they all silenced and turned in one massive pivot toward me.

The angel and I took our first morning meal, roasted peppers and bread made of mashed corn, which we dipped in wine. Every few minutes as we ate, the mass of beasts sounded and jostled for place, then quieted again. I simply didn't know how I would do this. Thousands of pairs of eyes were watching us, waiting. I grew more and more anxious. I looked over at the angel. It was dipping its bread in and out of its wine, watching the drops fall back into its tumbler. Was eating new to this creature?

I put down my food and stepped to the edge of our camp. I waded in amongst the animals, weaving between pairs and small groups or three, four, five of a kind. I moved further out into the great wave of life. Some of the creatures made noises of grunts, squeaks, coos; those nearest nudged me as I walked, running their heads or hindquarters up under my hands as I passed. After wading deep into the mass I knelt and stroked one small field dweller's soft pelt. Under my fingertips delicate ribs jumped up and down with each breath. "Mmmmm," I hummed quietly. This was new to me as I looked upon the tiny beast. Its movements as it curled in my palm with its nose exploring my wrist appeared to me as sounds of who it was. "Owsss," I uttered softly in response.

And so in this way, with the mouse, the naming began. I watched how each huddle of creatures acted together, the males, the not-males which I would come to know as females, and the youngest ones. "They are families," said the angel. "A family is a small group of two or more, usually a male and female that have young together."

As I sat, a weasel slid under my leg and emerged on the other side of my knee, creeping silently down my leg. "Eeezzz!" I cried in delight. A kinkajou turned its feet whichever way it chose to run, up or down the nearest tree. The mill-bear rolled, its thick pelt patting down the dust as its round face stared up in contentment at me. Each of these movements appeared to me as a sound, an utterance carved in the air, turning letters and language, shuffling them before me. I spoke the names and the angel wrote them down. I kept at it all night, naming one family of creatures after another. The moon provided light as it reflected off the streams and the white bark of trees. Fireflies sparkled all around us. Those named turned and trailed off as those still needing names arrived to take their places. Through the night and into the next day from that spot I named until the clearing, the trees, and the sky were empty, quiet, dusk.

"That is a start. Let us go," said the angel.

Within a dozen days, and as many nights, the naming took on a routine. The angel and I would walk from one spot to another. "Here is a good place; we will stop here," the angel would say. The animals would gather just as they did the first time, we would name for a handful of days, perhaps a few more, pack up and travel again.

But within time, moons, mists, and seasons, I came to feel overwhelmed and alone. I began to sleep more and more, remaining in my slumber well into the daylight hours.

The little talking the angel and I did was mostly it talking to me.

"In naming there is born a relationship, an oversight of care and keeping," the angel said in its flat tone.

The Maker had said as well, long ago, that all He had made was for me to enjoy. So here I was, His heir turned loose in the far reaches of my kingdom, a lonely nomad, spewing names to an angel.

I began to see that the animals I named had more than I. They had ones who would play with them or collect food; they had others. I was so obviously the only of my kind. I was alone in every herd. Was I the only one He'd ever made? Was I some sort of curiosity?

Since I had not seen a whole one like me, I began to look for parts of me on different animals. I searched for an arm or an elbow, an ear with a lobe attached to the side of a head.

"Surely there is a forehead around here somewhere," I said.

"What?" asked the angel.

"A forehead, a body part that looks like mine!"

"Why?"

"Because it might mean there will be another, another me."

I noticed how the body hair on a pig resembled my own.

"An animal that has a jaw lined with lips?" asked the angel. "I've never seen such a thing. Do you need rest?"

I worried that I was the test of a new sort of beast. Was I doing well? Would I always be the only one? This last question I voiced. The angel looked up from its list of names.

"There is me, the dog, The Maker. Your question makes no sense."

It was not a loss I felt, but an absence. This was a need I had discovered that I was sure I hadn't had before. Soon the work of naming became all that I knew for sure. So I buried myself in it.

I lived to name.

I made a long, low set of benches using stones and logs

tied with hemp on which I lay on my belly to name the smallest animals; ants, grasshoppers, centipedes, slugs, the angel silently scribbling. The tiniest of these traversed like me, to and fro in the dust, but used another's antennae for a guide or a pebble as a recognized landmark. Even these had developed a special liking for my effort and gathered together for observation at each spot we stopped. The entire land was on notice that I was at work. Some in hordes, others in formation while carrying carefully clipped bits of leaves in their tiny jaws, they would scout around the leg of my bench as I dropped their name upon them like the blessing from a dying father.

I moved my benches to the wet soil at the edge of a nearby lake. There I found the spider-crab. I began to adjoin parts of the names of other creatures or the land to traits of those before me. I named seed-shrimp and fish-lice whose homes were under long flat rocks. They would burrow leg over leg into the mud even as I begged them to climb into my hand. The design of these creatures fed both my understanding and despair. How unique I was in their presence, even beyond my size and my work of naming them. I was alone. Hovering over these water-dwellers, I completed them, sovereignly pronouncing their names.

Stacks of tablets full of names, written by the angel, were left at each spot along the way. A stack now sat in the mud at the end of my bench on the shore of a lake, but it seemed to mean little to those named. They did not understand, could not understand this monument to my effort.

As I had lay flat for months, I sat and soon stood, my posture and our location changing with the size of the creatures that came to be named. I took time off, but in my rest I grew anxious, seeing only unnamed beasts all around me. I could not help but begin again. Like the benches I had made for naming the smallest, I had fashioned a ladder in expectation of larger animals. The ladder now stood, tucked up against the outside of a shack I had built at this stop some moons before.

I had spent the day sitting back against the ladder, staring off into the air before me. Dusk was setting in just as I felt hot, steamy air cloud across my face, leaving behind a moist film. A split-hoofed, goat-like beast stood and stared back at me, chewing, waiting for me to get on with it. The creature was what I would come to call a dwarf-blue sheep. A certain flower it ate gave its hooves a blue tint. The creature moved its stare past me to the angel.

"I am weary of your stalling." The angel sat on a low tree branch staring down at me. I noticed that the bottoms of its feet had turned the color of dirt. "You complain too much."

"Then offer an answer for me," I said.

"You need to accept your place, here, doing this thing, just as I have had to do."

I stood and slowly replied. "Accept my place. How simple."

Fast but as if without moving, the angel stood next to me. Close. "Yes, accept your place. I was in heaven, I was in the Presence. And now I'm here with you."

"I guess your experience is being made greater," I replied.

The angel turned fully toward me, looking right at me. "Nothing like yours."

I turned and walked off. I was done for the night. I was done with this ever-budding, never-blooming conversation. I don't know where the angel went or if it slept. I didn't care. I found a spot at the base of two trees behind the shack to spread out until morning. I slept but I didn't rest.

In my dreams during those cycles of seasons, the endless traveling and naming, I would contrive strange and wonderful animals. Some would speak to me, "Name me next!" or "Why are you standing upright?" or "Where is your family?" Others would change colors. Still others would be oddly constructed with furry bodies, scaly heads, and great curved tusks like tree limbs; they would turn their heads and scoop my legs out from under me. I stirred fitfully and stammered in my sleep, grasping for names, as if my tongue were stuck to the roof of my mouth or were swollen and dumb. Pitching and turning, I snapped awake one afternoon to a tickle on my chest and found myself on my feet with the tail of an ostrich brushing me, its head and slithering neck laid over its back as it napped with me.

I became the worn and ragged Master of Naming. New sounds invented in my head spun out of my mouth. The angel looked up from writing, silent, with an expression that begged for a spelling. "Listen closer," I said, repeating the name, "it is written just as it sounds." I named one creature having given up hope, another in a panic that this would never end, and another while numb to it all. I was shaded from the sun, covered in a thick, crusty paste of sweat, dust, and spray from sneezing and snorting beasts.

Overwhelmed by hatred for the endless task, I made poor attempts to create a community of one. Besides the small shacks I put up at our stops, I began to collect a few strands of hair or feather from each animal I named. Using sap, I affixed these to the walls inside our shack. Dreading more sleepless nights, I would climb onto my ladder and up the side of the shack to catch one last glimpse of its brilliance as the sun sank behind the trees.

I awoke late on one of the last days, mid-afternoon, and could not lift myself to my feet. I lay in a heap, and spoke to the absence of The Maker. I demanded to know the purpose of this effort of naming. I filled my mouth with arguments.

I, the man, inquired of Him. The made examined The Maker.

"Why have you forsaken me?"

My voice was swallowed by the thick forest. I challenged Him to give me a reason to hope. The insects paused and started again.

"Why? I told You that I was not right for this task. What am I to find in being alone?" I panted as if I'd been running.

"I ask You!" I flipped onto my back, my arms and legs spread wide in the dirt. "I, the nameless giver of names!"

I brought my fist up to my chest in a thud as if striking a drum. "I'll listen and You tell me."

I wished I might find Him, come even to where He sat and look Him in the eye.

"This is your creature speaking. I am speaking, calling out to You. You must care for me! It is who You are!" I knew this of Him; at least, I knew I had known this of Him at one time.

I whispered now. My eyes closed. The sun beating down, the ground around me growing warm. "I am here. Where are You? I see the work of Your hands all around me. But You ... You ... You are only a memory."

I thought of my orchard, my dog, my home. I detailed for Him our lives together. I reminded Him of the joys. I told Him that I would be glad for the days past, days when morning and night were clear to me, and when I didn't know what it meant to be alone.

"It is I! The one You stood over, the grit from fitting me together still under Your fingernails. You worked all that day, from just before dawn, knitting me, spinning me up from the dust. In the night You called out and with a flutter and a rush the heavenly beings descended onto the grassy knoll, jostling for a spot, all wingtips and light. They gathered, silent as they leaned in to see this new creature. To see me. 'What is that fine fur?' asked one. 'Hair,' You said. The dog nosed his way into the crowd. Paws together, forward on his haunches he sniffed and licked my dusty cheek. There I was, the nameless one-of-a-kind lying there, a low heat rising, warming, naked. Flawless. It was then, in a final embrace, You lay across me. My chest rose as Yours fell. And with them You watched; impressed, holding all speech, immediately in love.

"Have You forgotten? In my aloneness I cannot. We sat by the fire and laughed together, jokes and wine, long afternoons and late evenings. It is I, the one You taught to identify the stars and ride the horse. How is it that You have left me to this bitter task of naming these ones, those whose name You could simply provide with the grass they graze? You have made all Your creatures with another like them, some carrying little ones on their backs. Even as they are together I am here alone, my face in the dust."

I let out a last groan and gave in to my tears. "Alone I am not Your glory!"

If He heard me and if He came, He stood over me and I did not know. If He heard me and if He came, it was while I slept.

Oren of Susa: Coming to Know

Spread out between us is a meal of roasted young goat, fresh yogurt, and warmed beets. Adam and I are reclining under the awning of his part of the house, outside his room, facing the sea. We are taking supper together for the first time. I am hoping to have a talk with him; it is what I want from the evening ahead, a talk about all of this.

Adam has pulled his hair back in a long braid and has tied it off with several pale rings. I ask him about these rings and learn that they are part of an animal. "There is no part of an animal that we do not use," he says.

After hearing of the naming I am surprised that Adam is at ease eating and disposing of animals.

"Do you remember naming the first goat?"

"No. Not specifically. There were so many beasts in the clearing at that first stop. So many of the animals that first morning were of similar construction; I assume I named the goat there, but I don't know."

I thought back to the fish I'd seen him cleaning several evenings before. "You seem at ease harvesting these animals."

"I am now, Oren, but that has not always been the case."

"What happened?"

"In the telling. You're getting ahead of us. I'll get to it."

I could push but I decide to be patient and wait for the story. I take another slice of goat, more yogurt. This is the first yogurt I've had since leaving Susa. This yogurt is tart and tangy, not sweet and creamy. It is a good change.

"Do you have any of the tablets—the ones on which the angel wrote the names?"

"No. I've often wished I'd kept one. I had one for a while, but I don't anymore."

"I suppose they are still stacked in Eden, stacked here and there," I say.

"Yes, I suppose they are. There is no reason to think otherwise. They are probably grown over with moss and vines. Likely they would appear as odd earthen towers."

I nod. "As would the shacks."

"Most certainly."

"Perhaps, once our story is told," I say, "someone will put together a group of seekers and go in search of the tablets."

"Even if they were found, the names were written in a script that would be very hard to decipher."

"What do you mean?"

"The language we use now bears no resemblance to the one The Maker and I spoke and used in Eden."

I hadn't thought of that, of the language changing. "So as you're telling me of your life in Eden, you're translating your experiences as you remember them."

"Yes. Remember, I am much older than I look."

It is easy for me to think of Adam as my peer. It is as if we were boys together and are now finding ourselves reunited as old men, one of us having left our village and had a wonderful adventure.

"The angel that helped you—it is said that angels have wings. Did the angel that helped you with the naming have wings?"

"Yes it did, but they were not large and feathered appendages like that of some peacock. They were not the central detail of the creature as you might think. They were sleek, without feathers or hair. They appeared to be ridged and smooth and they laid flat, recessed, the angels body formed to hold them. They gave the angel great speed, but if you were not looking for them, you'd not even have noticed the wings."

"What happened to the angel? Did you ever see it again?"

"The angel must have left at the end of the naming. Just as at the end of each day's work it always left. I don't know where the angel went. It did tell me that it was one of a great many like it."

"Created by The Maker, you think?"

"The Maker told me He made all things. I think He must have made the angels too."

Conversation falls silent for several minutes as we watch a flock of birds swoop over us and out to sea. A mass of a thousand or more birds with wingspans the height of a man. They fly from overland out over the sea and toward the sun. It is one of the beautiful displays of life that happens, more often here, near Adam's home.

"This Maker," I start, "this is unlike anything I've ever heard."

Adam looks at me, not spinning up an argument, just listening.

"The tale of a Maker would be enough, but there is not only that. This is a Maker whose feet were made dirty with the same dirt as men's."

"It is good to know my story is holding its meaning, Oren."

"When you were telling me about how you called out to The Maker," I say, "you reminded me of this fellow over in the village. Have you heard about him?"

"No, I don't think so. Who is he?" asks Adam.

"I don't know his name. I was told he was a wealthy farmer, a herdsman, but lost everything. His family is gone, dead. He has nothing but the clothes on his back, which are nothing more than rags. All was destroyed in one disaster after another. Everyone ignores him except for a few friends. He's trying to get The Maker's attention, but his friends think he's committed some great wrong and that is why The Maker isn't listening to him. They think The Maker is punishing him. But the man holds his innocence. They argue back and forth."

"No. I hadn't heard this," says Adam. "Sounds like an interesting person, this fellow."

"I saw him on the edge of the village the other day. I asked one of the market keepers about him." I pause, unsure how to state my question. "But here is what I don't understand, where I think you can help me, Adam. How do you, or this fellow, know that The Maker hears you when you speak to Him?"

Adam sets down his plate. "You are thinking about this Maker as if He's a man, Oren. The Maker is not a man. The Maker is the Deity. He is always and everywhere. I know He hears because I am sure He is there. This fellow you tell me of, he would not argue with these other men nor would he continue to speak out to The Maker unless he believed the same way."

I am struck again that Adam holds to such knowledge. His experiences have convinced him. I want more of this idea of a Maker.

"If The Maker made all," Adam continues, as if reading my mind, "then why would He not be involved in it? What maker doesn't care for that which he makes? He made me. He spent my early days with me. He hears when I speak out to Him."

"I find it difficult," I say. "I can't see The Maker. I can't observe Him."

"There are things that cannot be felt, tasted, and seen, Oren. I'm telling you about those things. You know about all the others."

The old gray dog comes from around the house and in under the awning, finding a spot next to Adam.

"I am not telling you some ancient tale that has no meaning, I am telling you about The Maker. I am telling you how He handed creation to me and how I failed to grasp it. That woman you met, the orphans that are sold in Susa, the naked and blind child — their tragedies are my own.

"I will tell you soon enough about how I allowed all this to happen. But know this. The Maker sees and sustains them. The Maker sees and sustains us. This goat was on our plates tonight because He saw to it."

"You've had experiences that led you to these ideas," I say. "I'm a scribe who grew up in Susa. My father was a scribe and his father before him. There has been only the writing of generations, their tablets stacked in closets. No mystery, no wonder. This is all I know."

"Are you done finding new things to know, Oren?" Adam sits and looks out at the light the sun has left in its path over the sea. "There is a great deal we cannot see. Our sight, our experience, these are not the sole tests of what is and what is not."

"I need proof of this Maker, of what you say."

"You do not need proof, Oren, or some observation. You will come in time to be convinced. You will know."

"I would very much like some confidence in what you are saying. You are a mysterious one, Adam. And that is if you are not out of your mind."

"I saw, Oren. I saw the perfect work of The Maker; I held it in my hands. And now I have faith. Even if I am not seeing Him anymore, I have faith He is still at work. You can see Him too, Oren. He is why you have anything good, your tablet house, prosperity, your place in society. The Maker still makes. And He is making you."

"I have to think about this," I say.

"I understand. I've had time, more time than I've wanted to think about my story."

"I do like the idea, this idea of a Maker who still has His fingers in His creation."

"Be careful, Oren. It is not an idea, some thing that I've conjured. Some consideration you can take or leave. It is a fact. We do nothing alone. We're capable of nothing without companionship. That was the point of the naming—so that I could see the meaning of being alone."

The meaning of being alone. I think of it as we sit together here at dusk by the sea. Adam gets up and lights a flame at the edge of the awning—soft, yellow light. And I think of the distance between myself and those I have loved.

And I think of this Maker, who Adam says is here with us.

Chapter Four

A Shape for a Soul

Adam."

It was Him!

I stepped down from my ladder and turned in the direction of His voice. The last creature had left. The last tablet of names lay at my feet, and the angel, too, was gone. Sunlight flooded the glen in which I had been working. He stood some distance away, among the leaves and vines. I could not see Him well but His voice rang clear. It was not easily forgotten. What was this He had said to me? I had never heard this word. It was a sound without meaning.

"Adam."

It had been tens of hundreds of moons since I had departed to do this task. "Are You speaking to me?"

"Yes. Adam."

I stood looking toward Him. "I don't know what that means."

He continued moving toward me, slowly through the branches, smiling.

"I, too, can name," He said.

He had come just as the last beast was leaving, a woolen mammoth in whose fur I'd been up to my elbows. Like all the rest, it had wandered off, freshly labeled and none the wiser or lacking for having met up with me.

I was in no mood for riddles. I had questions for Him. I had words for His ears to hear. Where had He been these last many nights when I had been so nearly broken? I might have wandered off myself, following the muddy rut in the under-brush, had He not uttered this new word to me.

He could see me, bathed in the sunlight. My torso was filthy with layers of dust heaped upon me by the flapping ears of elephants and the tails of river-horses. My legs were bruised and my knees swollen from seasons upon seasons of clumsy physical labor, being kicked by deer-types and other antlered beasts, or being knocked down by the swing of a crocodile tail or some unnoticed body part. My hands and feet were blistered, the former cut and scuffed from too much work and too little play. My mind, which I was not sure if He could see or not, was an empty chamber, like a pot scraped clean—thin, cracking, not able to take much more. And here He was, at the end of such a drubbing, coming to me with this new idea.

He came clear of the forest and motioned me to a patch of grass just back from where He had come. Not taking my eyes off of Him, I followed. I expected answers. No more secrets. No more being alone. But as I stepped off the worn trail and into the grass, its damp, cool cushion pulled me down. Exhaustion took full hold of me, deep at my core. He placed His arm under my head.

"Rest, Adam."

I looked into His eyes, reading the meaning in His face. Adam. Adam. In this He had finished the task. I felt sleep fall over me like a skein of wool. Every creature I had named had been found with at least one other of its kind. What did He mean in naming me? Had he other names that needed creatures?

It took some time before I could move it. And then it slid only a little. I was frightened, wondering what it was, a weight the size of a small log lying across my chest. Startled, I realized I could not feel my arm. More awake now I began to work it out. The weight on top of me was mine. I had woken with my arm lying across my chest, and it was still asleep. I slid it back down to my side. No dreams had come to me and I didn't think I had tossed or rolled in my sleep. It was odd to have woken in this position, but I did not give it more than a second thought. Sitting up, I found the fog of sleep was slow to lift. I was stiff in my back and side. I leaned forward, stretching, touching my toes.

The day was well along, the sun warming the dew. After lifting myself to my feet, I walked down to a pool I had noticed a day or two before. The pool was deep, like a kettle cut in the rock. Rays of sunlight rippled across the blue-green outcrops toward the bottom. I dove off a low ledge; the cool, clear water washed me as if I were shedding a skin. A raven flew over as I shook the water from my hair. I thought almost solely of food and drink.

Returning to my camp site, I felt rested and alone. It was clear that the animals had ceased coming. This job of naming was like a long, bruising trance I'd been snapped out of by being named myself, the only one of my kind.

I began to prepare a spot where I might put in a fire. I was hungry. I would cook some food, eat, and then set a course for home. If He came I would offer a meal to Him.

I paused now and again to stretch a muscle I had missed. With an armful of wood I glanced down at my spilled travel sack looking for my flint.

I stopped and turned.

He was there.

And He was not alone.

I stared as they came toward me. Any thought of food and drink were swept away. For there in His hand was another hand, like my own—much, much like my own—but slight, slender, not brutish and hard. A hand for calming, for finding concern and making it less so.

This new creature had been more precisely defined, more than any other—thin, delicate limbs, gentle curves, smooth like warmed wax. Hair was used as ornament, not covering. That on the head was long, gathered and held with a twisted flowering vine. My eye fell over the crest of a hip and was pulled down the smooth descent of a thigh.

I dropped the firewood. It clattered to the ground.

I had to force myself to slow down, to not move toward her, to not be dragged toward her by the energy of my tightening senses. All there was before me was this creature. Nothing else mattered to me. Before me was my clear and singular match.

My other one.

They came closer, this new one staring back at me, looking into my eyes. Other creatures I'd found interesting, an observation. But this one took me. This one pulled at me. My insides flushed, warmth rose in waves from my loins into my chest.

I felt overcome with the sense that I should say something, speak to this creature. I heard my breathing. I sounded like a panting hyena. I wanted to fill the air with something else. So I began to speak, I began to utter words to this creature, to Him, to all three of us.

"I was walking back ... I was just swimming ... when ... I was going to cook—" All that language, the deep well of sounds from which I had drawn for the naming, the forming, and arranging of letters, all I had mastered now failed. Fell short. I stopped and took a deep breath. "You are not like the others," I said.

Neither of them said anything, so I continued. "I was alone and now—"

It was then that He took another step closer, still holding her hand. Standing between us He lifted her hand in His, and He offered her hand to me. This hand He had made and held since its beginning. This hand He had loved more than would I.

He stood between us and spoke. "Once I found a piece of flint, it took only moments to gently twist, snap, and lift out your rib. I used spittle and dust to smooth it over, allowing the warm sunlight to set the thin wound off on its way to becoming a scar."

I found and felt the mark on my side, at my elbow. Running my fingertips over it, it seemed to me to be more of a scratch, as if I had rolled onto something or grabbed a tickle in my sleep.

He gestured and smiled as if He held in His hand a precious gem. "Raw material, this rib. I paced, slowly twirling it between My fingers." He looked at me. "You were lying several paces away, at My feet, asleep."

She listened, looking now at The Maker as He spoke and then back at me.

"The rib warmed in the palm of My hand, softening to putty. So I pulled and I stretched it thin and I formed a shape. A shape for a soul I have long imagined."

Her hand remained in His. Deep brown, her hand was so fine and thin—He might leave fingerprints if He squeezed. She looked at my hand hanging at my side and at me. She had not smiled. She had made no move toward me.

Then she looked up into His face and I heard her first words.

"So this is him?"

Silence.

He looked at me.

"Adam," I said, as if knocked awake. "I am Adam."

The name He had given came from my mouth for the first time. I was set apart from all else, labeled among all creation. The name made it clear that I was a man of the soil and the dust.

"Is this your home?" She looked around the spot where I had slept so many nights out in the open like a beast, our last stop, the shack, the ladder, my low bench with one leg missing.

"No ... no," I stammered, "I'm traveling. This is just where I stopped for a few nights."

My crumpled knapsack was spilled on the ground, its contents everywhere. I was like a monkey, encircled by his own dung.

"Where is home?" she asked, still standing close to Him.

"It is a day or two from here by foot," I said. I had no idea how far it was back to the house. "I was just planning to head back there. I need to get back. Much there needs me."

She made no reply. I had no idea what to say next, but I heard myself continue talking.

"I need to get back. Perhaps you ... would you like to go with me?"

I extended my hand now, surprising myself with this sudden confidence. The question hung, suspended, like the seed of a milkweed on an updraft at the base of a waterfall. There was no reason for her to accept the invitation. All she knew was my name and that I had slept on the ground last night and untold nights before that. I had at least bathed.

She looked again at The Maker and back at me with the start of a smile. Then, looking down at her feet she pulled back a strand of hair, tucked it behind one ear, and stepped forward. Her foot shuffled on the ground, her toes pushing dust onto mine.

She stood with me and we looked at Him as He laid her hand in mine.

I didn't know what to do with her, but I felt such glory standing there, sharing a patch of dirt with such a creature. Her hand felt soft and warm. She leaned into me, close. The air she brought with her was like spring water and cinnamon.

I looked at The Maker. He stood back. His eyes filled. His hand hung at His side, empty.

"Good," He said.

He turned and passed into the brush, pausing only once to see us standing, looking after Him.

And He was gone.

I scrambled about at her feet, on my hands and knees, picking up my supplies and pushing them into the sack. As I did, she lifted an arm and stretched. Her shadow fell over me. I stopped, turned, and looked up. A bronzed arm blotted out the sun. My gaze found its way up her perfect pillared neck.

I saw her look down at me, my reflection in the cocoa of her eye. She, I thought, in my care. At my blurted suggestion He had simply left her to me.

Left us to each other.

She watched as I gathered the last items and stuffed them into the dirty, scuffed sack. I stood and tied it shut, brushing the dirt from my hands.

"I can carry it," she said, taking the sack from me.

It looked like a rotting wineskin as it sat in the crook of her elbow, her fingers wrapped around it.

"Let me," I said. "You are not a beast meant to carry a bag."

I saw a shock of lilies just off to the side. I bent and with both hands I broke off a bundle of stems.

"I'll trade you," I said.

I lifted the sack and dropped the flowers in her arms. She looked at the flowers. She then bent down in the grass. Laying them out, she began arranging the blooms, braiding their long stems and tying them together with a blade of grass, one at the top and one at the bottom.

I watched her do this and wondered what sort of creature is made to do such a thing? He had formed her from me, but she was something else altogether. As she stood with the bouquet, all the life around us was completed under her gaze.

"You have some experience with flowers," I said.

"Only now. These are the first I've held close like this. I saw they needed some tending after you dropped them into my arms."

What else do you know? I thought as I moved closer to her. She was only a little shorter than I was.

"Your voice, it is soft and light," I said. I touched her neck and she hummed. I could feel the vibration.

"I was without you," I said.

"He said you were looking."

"But I did not know what I was looking for," I said. "I couldn't have known."

I saw her gaze drop to my elbow. I lifted my arm and looked down. She put her hand to my side. Her fingertips on the scar, I felt my skin come alive under her touch. I felt an energy, a desire that I didn't understand. It was time to leave.

"I'll show you my house," I said as I put my arm around her, just under her shoulder and across her back. Again she lifted a strand of hair and put it behind one ear as together we turned for home.

"Will you bring me back?" she asked.

"If you want to come back, yes, I will bring you back."

As we descended toward the valley her hair brushed across my shoulder. Just hours before I couldn't imagine her. Now I couldn't imagine this place without her. I leaned in, her ear at the tip of my nose, and just above a whisper I said, "You ... and I."

Oren of Susa: Concubines in Pairs, Walking!

"Care to go for a swim?" Adam asks, "in the sea?" "I have never gone swimming in the sea. I don't think so."

"Oh? You should. It's very refreshing, cleansing even. Come along. I have a raft. You can sit on the raft while I swim if you don't want to swim."

I put my bare feet in the water as I sit on the edge of the raft. The water is cool, not quite cold. I look down and can see nothing beyond my toes. I am used to seeing the bottom, rocks washed clean by the current of the river. But here there is nothing, just darker and darker blue—hues turning to black. We are afloat on the surface of The Maker's sea. Each wave lifts and drops the raft, soft rises and falls, rocking up and down. What causes this constant movement? I imagine The Maker's energy infusing, causing each ripple to sprout, to push up. Still, I can't imagine putting my entire body in this water. I'm not ready for that. I know there are creatures in there. And I have no idea how to move myself through water where I cannot touch the bottom.

Adam strips to swim. The sun is bright and hot. I shield my eyes from it with my arm and look over at him. As he lets himself down into the water I see it. A dark streak, a blemish, the skin pulled tight around it. It is longer that I imagined. Seeing it makes it almost real. Adam has a scar running along his side where The Maker cut him open.

The memory of Eve is carved in his flesh.

I am not sure how to ask. "I ... may I ..."

Adam turns toward me, almost as if he's not sure I said anything. "Yes?"

"I don't want to trouble you, but—"

Adam stops me."You want to touch the scar?"

"Yes. How did you guess?"

"You are far from the first to ask, Oren." He settles back on the raft and half-turns his back to me, his arm lifted slightly. "Go ahead. Feel what you see. Know for yourself."

I put my fingertip to the scar. The old skin sags, soft to my touch, while the skin nearest it looks pink and perfect like a baby's. There is a slight indention that runs the length of it.

I pull my hand away. Adam says nothing. He lowers his arm, puts his hand to the raft, and lifts off into the water.

He floats in the water just off the raft, the ripples breaking around him.

"You mentioned, when you came and met me at the tablet house, that Eve is now gone."

"She is dead, Oren. You can say it."

I don't want to say she is dead. It is too difficult. I have known such a death and I don't like giving it recognition by naming its deed.

"Dead." I rush past it. "How long has it been?"

"Nearly three harvests," says Adam.

He turns, puts his head down, and vanishes under the surface of the water. I see his feet for a moment then I don't. I feel a tinge of fear. Bubbles stop surfacing. I doubt I can get this raft to shore by myself. Then there is a movement of color from deep down. A brown form. A face, then eyes on the face. He breaks the surface. I am shocked to see that he kept his eyes open under the water.

He swims back and forth in front of me.

"And have there been others since her?" I ask.

"Other women?"

"Yes."

"No."

"None at all?"

"No. Certainly not. If you had seen Eve, if you had met her and talked with her you would see the foolishness of your question."

"What do you mean?"

"There is no woman since Eve. Not for me. All women since her are but reflections of a woman, Oren."

I think of the two women I have known. I can't imagine Adam has been with no other women. "I see."

"I doubt you do. What is on your mind?" He floats up and hangs, resting on the corner of the raft.

"After supper the first evening I was here, I went walking. I walked the paths at sunset. There were pairs of women. I think I saw six pairs of them. They were all wearing colorful wraps and were quite lovely."

"Only reflections."

"Well to me they were beautiful enough."

"So?"

"As I finished my walk, after the sun had set, I was wondering about them."

"Speak freely, Oren."

"Are these your concubines, Adam?"

He pushes himself out from the raft and stops swimming, hanging in the water right in front of me, he doesn't seem to move at all.

"You think that I live out here by the sea with my bevy of servants and that I keep a house full of women to carry me through my oldest age and toward my death, women to comfort me after the exit of my Eve? The one He made for me, the one He made me for?"

"I suppose so. I have no reason not to think such a thing."

"No, Oren. These are my servant's wives. I might guess that one or two of the women may have been a daughter or granddaughter of one of them. I don't keep track anymore. In any case, no. I don't keep women to try to fill the void Eve left. That would not be possible."

"I see. I didn't realize," I say.

"I am satisfied with the loss of Eve," he says, pulling himself back up onto the raft.

He wraps his cloak back around himself and picks up the oar. We begin moving slowly toward the shore.

I don't understand. Satisfied with the loss? I've certainly tried. I've tried to fill the void that was left after my loss. No matter his age, how can a man not? I look out; the sea ripples into the horizon. Has The Maker done that for him too? Fashioned for him such contentment?

Chapter Five

In Terms of Wonder

I felt her hand in mine, the warmth between us. She had woven her fingers through mine, interlocking, each finger held secure. What a different return than I could have conceived. I had always thought that this place I had made was too large for me. I could not have dreamed ... yet here she was. I wanted to show her all I had discovered, designed, and built; to show her my fields, vines, and my wine press.

"Here we are," I said. "This is my home."

We slowed to a stop. The flowering vines I'd planted around the house had nearly covered it in gold and blue flowers and the trees nearby had grown to hang close over it.

"Our home," I said. "Our house."

"Where did it come from? Did He make it?"

"I made it. I made it so that I would have a place, like all the creatures have their own place."

She let go of my hand and took a few steps forward.

"Do you like it?" I asked.

"Very much. It looks like a place from here, like it grew up from here."

"Good." That was how I'd always seen it too. And I'd made room for her, not knowing of her at all. "I made it with room for you too."

"So you want me to stay?"

I put my arms around her and pulled her to me. "I give it to you. It is yours." I held her against me. As I did she lifted her arms and put them over my shoulders. I laid my face to the side of hers and breathed in the air where her hair dropped onto her shoulder. For the first time I put my lips to her skin. Her perfect neck under the press of my lips lifted me. All else around me was blotted out by my desire, which was surpassed only by thanksgiving to The Maker for her. I felt as if I could remain there, attached to her until the end of time, until the scar-tree was whittled away from all my marks upon it. I heard her breathe in, sharply, and press her neck into me. I wanted to kiss her neck, down and around, past her hair and down the center of her back.

But not yet.

I pulled myself up straight in front of her again. "Here. Let me show you some more of this place."

I took her hand again and we ran around to the storehouse where I had left to dry fruits, herbs, and spices. All were hung in fragrant rafts over our heads. Inside, the smells wafted together. The air was rich and cool, the earth soft against our feet. Above us a bough of apricots was drying.

"Lift me up," she said.

I bent, wrapped my arms around her knees and lifted her into the air. As she went up, she giggled. It was a sound I'd never heard. I wanted to hear it again. It carried in its jingle what this creature was, her playful essence. Her way of seeing and taking what she wanted. As I helped her up, my chin at her hip, this sound was like a call to me. She pulled one of the apricots and brought it down with her, tearing at the fruit with her teeth and eating it. And as I sat her back down in front of me she grabbed onto me and put her lips on mine. Her hands at the back of my head, she kissed me with her whole self, her curves pressed warm, filling the spaces against me. In the soft grass, in the shade of the storehouse, we found that we fit together. We were made for each other. There was no fear, no waiting to see. He had made us for us, one for one.

Although I tried to impress her, I soon saw more in her. I saw in my mate a woman, a creature He had made to go with me. She was capable, lively, and thoughtful. She brought a certain understanding, a way of looking and seeing that I did not have ... still don't have.

Within our first days together she made my home her own. She moved easily about making changes to our habits. She began bringing plants and vines into the house. One of these flowering plants I had seen before. It was the one she had worn in her hair when I first saw her.

She made clay troughs and took cooking herbs from the storehouse and brought them inside, bundles of them tied in bows of woven horse hair. She surprised me with a wax and wick which she used to light our room at night. This house became a place where we found out how to be always together. My life with The Maker and discovering the birth land, this all appeared now to have been only a start. Indeed, all that had come before was only the beginning, the time of waiting for her.

We slept outside many evenings. Often on these nights we would lie awake and talk.

"He told me of the distance between the lights," I said.

She looked up into the sky and listened.

"He told me that some of them He hung with care in the spot He'd prepared for them, while others He flung joyfully into the void, arcs of fiery white light streaming as they crossed over and passed each other."

"What keeps them there?" she asked.

"I don't know."

"I think I do. His desire. His simple want is what keeps them there."

We listened to the birds as they sang together and circled us, rising in spirals into the darkening sky. As we did I heard her breathing fast, in spurts. I looked over and saw her lips puckered as if to kiss the air. She was blowing a stream of air up at the birds. She kept moving her lips in and out, up and down.

"What is it?" I asked.

She kept going, ignoring my question. What was she doing? Then I heard a sound come out of her. It was not a squeak or a shout; it was a call, a tone. The birds, she was making the song of the birds! She was imitating them. Their spiraling began to descend. They came down, settling in the trees around us, chirping in rhythm, back and forth with each other and with her. I had never had the thought, the idea to imitate an animal, to call to a creature like that. I watched her sing with the birds that night.

"I woke to find myself cradled in His arms. He held me as I began to breathe and lift my eyelids against the light." She was telling me of her birth.

She had awakened to Him with much the same feelings I had, but with a greater feeling of being close to another, a desire she would carry with her for the rest of her days.

"As He stood me up for the first time, He walked with me, watching my footsteps, ready to catch me. He once put His hand on my back to stop me and bent in front of me, removing a rock that sat in my path."

"He taught you to walk?" I asked.

"Next to Him." She nodded. "And He did catch me. I once leaned too far toward a piece of ripened fruit. He plucked me out of midair, rolled me into His arms, and cradled me until we'd both caught our breath. He then set me down again on my feet."

I scooted close and put my arm around her. My dog curled at her feet rather than mine. If I'd been him I would have done the same. She reached down and rubbed his neck. Together we slept, under the sky, and the sunlight warmed us as we woke.

Days were spent in long walks, what we came to call hikes, or in swimming together. We fed each other berries and sipped the milk of deer. I made her a swing of vines with a piece of slate as a seat and pushed her. She soon learned to move her legs, sailing over my head, lifting away from me and coming down again, that giggle echoing.

After hiking to the edge of the river one afternoon, I pulled her down into the tall grass and kissed her; her wrist, her forehead, each hip and joint.

We lay there together in the sun.

"Love."

"What?" I said.

"I love you," she said.

I looked at her and watched the words roll from between her lips again. "I love you."

"Love," I repeated. "Yes, I love you ... I love you too," I said.

It was a word we couldn't define. But it came to us and we used it to explain the depth of our delight, our life in each other. We found it and saved it for the expression of this, the finishing of ourselves as he and she in the other. One.

And we lived like no one since. We came to know and care for all the life around us. Every plant and creature was good. Taking and giving in balance. Every leaf lifted on every breeze. There was no waste, no loss, not a tear was shed. We lived like no one since.

I showed her all I had discovered, designed, and built. I told her how I picked the stones for the arch and how they fit together. She stepped up close to the arch and tried to push her fingertip into the crevice between two of the rocks. She then came and stood next to me so that our bellies were pressed together. She took her fingertip again and tried to push it between us. And then she moved her finger around to my side and found the indention from where The Maker had cut into me. "Like us." she said.

I taught her to make wine, though she had no taste for it. I told her of naming the animals and of the angel and I showed her one of the tablets with the names written on it, the only one I kept. "There are stacks of them out there," I told her.

There was almost nothing I knew that I did not in time tell her. Almost. The tree I wanted to keep. I wanted to keep it for myself. I didn't want to bring it along with me into this new life with her.

But I kept giving her a little bit more. I kept trying to satisfy her desire to know while also trying to find a place where I could stop the story. Leave it as it is.

I started to tell her about a hike The Maker and I had taken. "Overnight ... we hiked far to the other side of Eden. The path took us across streams, under waterfalls ..." But the story turned from a story about a hike into a story about the hike. The one.

"What was there? Why did He take you that far for that long?"

This beautiful woman, all her attention was on me and my experience. She looked at me and listened with desire for my answer.

I fed her little bits at a time, insufficient details.

I should be holding back, I thought. I should be telling her none of it. These thoughts, this dialogue with myself, ran along under the conversation with her.

"There was a tree."

"A tree? What about it caused Him to take you there?"

Her questions were pulling the story, unraveling it from my grip. "The bark was unfeeling ..." She does not need this story. It is nothing good.

I was losing the story to her. It was like I was sliding down a steep riverbank. "A fruit grew from it."

"What kind of fruit?"

"I didn't eat it." Was this defense or detail?

"Why not?"

"It was not good."

"What do you mean it was not good?"

"He told me to leave it as it was."

I had said the words—leave it as it was—but they did not carry weight. They did not slow her down. They did not mean to her what they meant to me.

"Why?"

"He said all is not good, that there is something else." I was failing to tell her all The Maker had said. My attempt to leave out details this late in the story was only raising her interest.

She stood and looked at me. "He took you to see a tree that was unlike any other and told you not to eat of it because it is not made good?"

"Yes. The one fruit that I picked I left sitting in a mud of its own juice."

Why did I not stop talking?

"You picked one?"

"Yes."

I looked away from her at the clear blue sky. Leave it as it is. My gut felt tight. I'd gone too far, said too much. I had told her the one thing I didn't want to tell her, the one thing I wanted to keep hidden away so it could do her no harm.

She was excited, curious. "This is a tree I want to see for myself! Will you take me there?"

And this tree became important to her as it was a part of Eden that she had not yet seen. Almost nightly she mentioned the tree. Long after I had brought it up the first time, she continued to speak of it. In terms of wonder she would ask after it, desiring to know all that had been made by His hand. Of course she knew, for I had told her. What she wanted was to know—to experience.

"Will you tell me about its leaves again?"

And I would tell her.

"The air was cool in the shade? It was cool and the light was dim?"

And I would tell her.

"There were no birds in the tree?"

And I would tell her.

No matter how much I said in an effort to exhaust her curiosity, she would return to it.

One evening I lay on my side, my back to her.

"I want to see the tree for myself," she said.

Her tone was no longer one of asking, she had turned her mind to her goal of knowing. I felt the words as I heard them. Her mouth was against my ear, her arm draped around me, her fingertips resting on my thigh.

This was nothing I didn't already know. "I think I was asleep," I said, slowly opening my eyes.

The insects were in full chorus. Moonlight formed shadows across our mat of stuffed-down and woven water-grass.

"We will leave you to sleep."

I made no response. How could I be in the minority? Was I being left out? Was I somehow missing conversations she was having with Him?

"We?" I asked.

"I asked Him to take me to the tree of knowing. He said I should ask you. I told Him that I have worn myself out asking you."

I rolled onto my back, saying nothing. She took this opportunity to come close to me. All she wanted was to be near me, to know what I knew. Raising herself on one elbow, she lifted her smooth, tanned leg over me. Her warmth began to melt me as her lips found my neck. I pulled her against me. She had only good to give to me.

I had long decided that the place where the tree stood should remain a memory. My memory. I wanted to leave it in the past, that cold bark, the heft of the fruit and the spice of the nectar; I wanted to leave it there in the dust.

Lying there with her, I felt no pangs of panic or loneliness and I wanted her to never feel what I had felt. She should never see that place. She was in my care. Going to that tree, under its canopy, there was a thing under there that would not love her like I did.

She lay next to me, her hand on my chest. "Your memory has made more of it than it was."

"No it hasn't," I said. "Memories, like everything around us were made by Him. They are good."

So once again I gave her the story. "We walked a night and a day. At times I was asleep on my feet."

"And your dog did not come?" she asked.

It was more than I'd ever said. "Right. But it was easy to forget myself once I was under the tree. It was not as much a tree as a place. An entry. As I stood at its trunk I felt like

I was standing at a door, a gate. The fruit of the tree, as I've told you, was like juicy granite. It fell to the ground, forming a crater in the dust. His words were clearer than they'd ever been. 'Leave it as it is.'"

"He said nothing else?" she asked.

"He said that what I was seeing of this tree, of this place in its shade was all I should ever wish to see. And I could tell that while I was amazed and amused by the tree, He understood, and He didn't care to linger with me in its shade."

"He told you not to go near it? Not even to touch it?"

"He said not to taste it."

The next night I went to bed before she did. I fretted over giving in to her. I pushed the possibilities about in my head like I was choosing between stones. Her desire was only to know; maybe if she saw the spot with me, while I showed it to her, maybe she would be able to imagine hearing His words and seeing the action. Perhaps we could go past it and I could simply point it out as we rode by. Maybe then the story I had told her would make itself visible. I had said no to her out of concern for what might be, and because I believed, still believe, no was the right answer.

She came in, leaving the room dark.

"You should get some sleep. From what you say of the trip, you should certainly get some sleep." She spoke as if a decision had been made.

She slipped into the bed next to me.

How did she know I was not already asleep?

"The trip is not the half of it, I assure you," I replied. I rolled over and kissed her. "The place is everything you have already seen, and nothing you can't imagine."

This was ridiculous. I had already spoken of the place too much to suggest such a thing.

"Then what is the matter with it?" she quizzed again. "Take me there and bring me back. What can be the loss in that?"

I had no new words.

I silently gave in.

Maybe she was right. Maybe it was just me. Maybe I had made too much of it. What loss was I protecting? Why was I being so stubborn, soaked in caution?

She was right. I should get some sleep.

This time I won the debate. We took the horse. I was not going to undertake such a journey on foot again, as I had with The Maker. I had managed to sleep only a little. We were up and on our way before I had come fully around. I was in no hurry. I would have to find the way. I knew the general direction and I thought I knew which region and grove; landmarks were fresh enough in my mind.

Soon the sun swung into its place directly overhead. The young man who had first come this way seemed not like me, but like a boy I'd once known who had run off and vanished into the mist. The trail The Maker and I had taken before was barely visible; the plants that grew in it were half-height, allowing me to spot it only bit by bit as we went.

"This spot looks like another we passed before," she said.

I recognized the error and grew more tense and uneasy.

"That is because it is," I said with a sharper edge than I meant. "Here ... right here is the path. That climb back there threw me off."

"Is the horse leading or are you?" She laughed at her joke.

Her talk of scenery and her joy of traveling grated on me.

"Why don't we tour more often? There is so much of this place we've never seen."

Her breath on the nape of my neck, her excitement only drove my anxiety. I focused on the ground, watching it as the afternoon made shadows and the sun strolled down our backs.

We stopped just after dark to rest. She said she wished to bathe in a pool we had just passed. I was ready to stop so I turned the horse back. A quiet brook came down the rocks and trickled over the rim of a deep pit cut into the rock, the walls of which were heavily layered with quartz. The pool glowed, as if it were floating in the dark earth. The white rock seemed to bend under the water as she floated above it, the moonlight in flickering ripples all around her.

Oren of Susa: She

Adam and I are taking a late afternoon walk by the sea. Actually, Adam is taking the walk. His mood is thoughtful and reflective. I am several paces behind him, listening for any details he might offer, details I may have left out of the telling.

The task of telling has gotten more difficult for him. I have seen it in his posture; in the way he sits limp in the chair or puts his legs straight out in front of him and lets his head fall back in silence. It is not like earlier in the telling when he raced along telling me the story. He is full of pauses as he speaks of her, pauses during which he sits quietly and thinks thoughts that will never be known. There are many moments when I wonder if I shouldn't offer to halt the work and pick back up in a day or two.

An hour ago he simply stood up and left the room—not in anger or frustration, more like he had remembered some task he'd meant to do. I followed him.

"I know that was our last night, the last night we would be able to sleep so well. It was the last night with nothing in the space between her and me."

I take several fast steps to catch up with him. "You regret taking her to see the tree."

Adam slows to a stop. The water breaks at our ankles. He looks down as if the past is written in the sand at his feet, as if he can simply read it to me. He speaks with both a deep familiarity of what happened and awe for the facts, made new and fresh in the telling.

"The place had become a part of me and she wanted part of it as well. She was curious. It seems right as I say it. It seems innocent because it was." He looks at me. "It was innocent."

"But you did question it." My voice low and even, pushing for more. "Even as she swam you questioned going."

"Her swim ... at the time it was another stop on a trip that could not be over soon enough. I was not questioning. I was looking past the trip. I wanted it over."

As he speaks I can see the loss of this woman in the worn, leathery skin of his face, in the long gray strands of his scalp, in the rise then drop of his gaze.

"Of course," I say.

He continues. "But now it is a memory lodged deep within me, a desire once satisfied, a joy once held. If I could stand at the edge of that pool once more ..."

I follow as Adam walks up the beach, away from the water, and sits in the tall grass. "I bring to the surface such old pleasures, Oren, the last time her beauty was bare, available to me, to all creation."

I sit down next to him. "I am sorry, Adam." I say this, not to be kind, but because I know. I know something of this—this terrible looking back as an old man.

Two boats float on the horizon. Perhaps they are market boats moving between ports. Their sails are slack; the breeze has stopped here too, dead air.

"Has there ever been a woman for you, Oren?"

He is looking at me and I am certain the look on my face is closed—my head slightly back as if to say that none of this is supposed to be about me. I don't care for the questions coming in my direction. But he waits and he has given a lot and deserves an answer.

"Yes. Her father and mine were scribes in Susa. They went to the same tablet house as boys."

"You knew her a long time then."

"We were born the same spring. They used to say that we learned to walk the following winter just so we could meet each other."

Adam smiles. "You were very close then."

"And we were together until the summer after I was apprenticed."

"Tell me, Oren." Adam looks at me thoughtfully. He has switched places and has become the scribe for a few moments. The memories are familiar but become new and strange again as I narrate them, the telling, the testifying— yes, we have switched places.

"One summer evening I borrowed my father's horses to take her for a sunset ride. Instead of walking them down the road into the forest or taking the path to the well and back, we rode the horses out the other way and were soon racing back and forth across the open fields to the eastern edge of the village. We made several passes and loops until it was nearly dark and the beasts were tired."

"Lovely," says Adam.

"I walked my horse up along the side of hers. I gave her a kiss. 'It is nearly dark,' I said. 'We should go back.'

"'A bit longer, let's ride a bit longer.'

"I looked up at the light. The open field stretched all around us. Sounds from the village carried across the tall grass, the voice of a herdsman driving his flock in for the night, someone chopping wood. The hum of locusts rose from the trees along the road. A mother called her children inside.

"I kissed her again and as I started to pull away she lunged forward and kissed me as she laughed. She was happy, at this night and at being with me. I felt joy, a command and a delight as if I ruled the world. I spurred my horse and he took off. She put her heels into her horse as well and sprinted after me. I turned in full gallop to look back at her, to see her hair floating behind her as she gained on me. But instead I turned and saw her smock billowed up. I saw her horse drop out from under her and the heels of her shoes pointed toward the plum-colored summer sky.

"I pulled up so hard that my horse bellowed. I turned back, jumped down and ran to her. My horse stomped and pranced near where her horse laid on its side, breathing in shallow puffs, its one leg turned hoof up and out. She had hit a stump, cut mere inches off the ground just behind us in the trampled grass.

"I fell on my knees next to her. 'Liana! Liana!' Her head was twisted too far to one side and at an angle I still see when I close my eyes. One of her arms was crumpled under her and the other was splayed out as if relaxed but for her forearm—which was folded up and back, away from the grass, her hand hanging limp at the end of it. Even in that low light I could see that her face was slack and ashen, her eyes filled with dusk, staring lazy and empty at the dirt. I began to shake and sob. The village watchmen had heard me cry her name and soon a huddle of them was moving across the field toward us, rushing under a pool of torchlight.

"And coming along at some distance beyond them, I could make out the silhouettes of our fathers."

Adam and I are both quiet for several minutes. The memory of that evening is a rut I have worn in my past—like a pacing beast, back and forth I've gone so many times. I wonder if Liana has been given more of my thought than she would have if she had lived. If she were an old woman in my house, the mother of my children, perhaps I would have thought of her less. At this pause in the telling of our stories—Adam's many ruts and my few—silence seems a proper response.

"Many times have I thought of that pool where Eve swam," says Adam. "Did you ever go back to the spot where she fell?"

"Yes. I did, but there aren't fields there anymore. It was long ago swallowed up by the village. There is now some structure or a street there. Someone's smokehouse or the curb of some alley marks the spot where she laid."

"So the place is only in your memory."

"Yes, I carry it with me, a field of regret."

Adam stands and offers his hand to help me up.

"You and I, Oren, we're men of loss."

I take his hand and pull. I stand next to him.

"Eve and Liana," he says.

Chapter Six

Aware We Were

We arrived at the tree very late that night. Morning was not far behind us. I was so tired and burdened by the journey, had the horse ridden me, I'd not have known the difference.

I saw the tree from a distance. I recognized it at once. It was like a great sculpture towering, casting a shadow that an entire village could have gathered within. It stood as if it had swallowed all the plants around it and now looked on the rest with greed.

"If this isn't it, it must be one of its seed," she said as we slowed.

"No, this is it."

Either my memory had failed or the tree had grown larger, swelled so that the path was now under it. The air in its shadow was damp and still, filled with the thick smell of earth and citrus. That same hulking trunk gave way to great beams, twisting and shooting off at this angle and that. All led to the leaves, just as I remembered them, with their stretched, lifeless pale-green hue. I caught myself looking behind us as I walked the horse further up the path under the edge of the tree's canopy. Was He here as well, standing off, watching us? I did not stop. She slid down off the horse in mid-stride. I heard the tree's limbs creak as if in response, as if welcoming her into their shade.

She looked up as she walked in under the tree. "This is amazing. It is ... it is just as you said!"

I rode a few more paces, trying to suggest with this simple action that we needn't tarry. She was not watching me. I stopped and turned, watching her go. She held a lit wick in one hand which gave me her silhouette, an edge of her moving away from me. I remained on my horse, shifted my weight, and looked around. I waited and grew nervous with the thought that He might see us.

"So," I called, "now you've seen it."

I watched her outline in the light as she moved toward the trunk. I watched her disappear, as if the light had gone out, only to reappear again on the other side of the trunk several moments later.

"There is a waterfall nearby," I said. "Do you hear it? Let's build a fire, eat, and rest the horse."

She was further from me than she'd ever been. I should follow her, I thought. She is alone under there. This is not a good place for her. This is not what I intended when I gave in to her to come here.

Leave it as it is.

I felt like He was whispering in my ear even now. I jumped and turned, staring wide-eyed into the starlit brush. The waterfall splashed on the rock somewhere behind, gurgling. A frog called out once, twice ... the sounds of His making.

Then I heard her.

I could not decipher words, only the rise and fall, the pause and phrase as if listening to voices from across a valley. She seemed to be talking to herself, as if in conversation. I leaned down and laid across my horse's mane, peering under the overhang of the great tree. I heard her again. I watched as she pulled the wick in close. I could see her face, the side of her face in a circle of light deep under the tree. She spoke as she studied a branch that was heavy with fruit. Several of the bulbs hung around her, the light from her wick against their ivory skins. I watched her fingers brush the bark, caress one leaf and then another. Grabbing a branch, she paused and pulled herself close as if listening to it.

"Won't you come?" I said, not loud enough.

But then I saw her turn and playfully throw a piece of the citrus to me. Surprised, I reached as the pale bulb glanced off my fingertips and slid into the brush on the other side of the trail, landing hard among some young briar sprouts.

I came down off my horse and stepped across the path, slowly. I watched her; her back to me, she picked fruit, pausing, looking at and picking another. She was turned full to the tree, but I could still hear the sound of her voice. Was she talking to the tree?

I was on foot under the canopy of the great tree for the second time. There was a fruit lying in the dirt, a dried-up hull. Could it be the very piece I had picked so long ago? It caused me to stop for a moment, but I was determined to go in after her. I continued through the cool shadow, trying to hear what she was saying. I was able to hear only some of the words even as I stopped to listen. Were those her words?

But she was now still. Was she also listening? Who was she talking to? What was she doing? I saw that the wick lay tipped and snuffed in the dirt, the not-quite-white wax spilled as if spewed from the blackened stub.

His words hung far in the back of my memory. "Life can be taken away, slowly replaced with dry stillness. Dust without breath."

I came around to her side. As I did, she turned full toward me with a smile and a piece of the fruit. She held it up to me between the palms of her hands. Through a slit, the nectar beaded up, released, and ran down between her fingers and down the back of her hand. The smell of it was like always, like forever. I wanted to soak in it. And now even more—the scent, the sweetness of it on her, on her beauty. I felt a desire completed.

I smiled in return as I stood close to her, my lover. "Who were you talking to?" I asked, breathing deep the nectar. "I heard you but there was only the tree—"

And then I saw. Hanging onto the trunk of the tree, was a little dragon. That is what I called it after, long after: dragon. I did not recognize this elegant creature. I didn't think I'd seen one. I was sure I hadn't named it.

Its tail and body were not quite equal in length. The entire creature was no longer than my forearm. It had a jagged jawline that led down to a strong muscular core and legs with feet that ended in claws. Its silver-gray tone stood out against the bark. The first strands of dawn reflected a rich, scaly blue stripe running from its snout to the tip of its tail. It had stopped at eye-level, its head pointed and its neck angled up as if it were one of us. It drew me in, the wisdom that hung behind its eyes—green half moons pulled in under bony brows—eyes that followed mine as I looked at her and back.

I kept my voice low, speaking to her, aware we were not alone. "You have seen it. This is it, my—"

Her fingers pressed soft to my lips. I could smell the nectar on her. My jaw tightened and my lips rose in a pucker against the sweet sticky print of her finger. Her eyes locked with mine as she lifted the fruit, tore back its skin, and playfully rested the bulb on her chin. I felt concern. A rising, a tinge, an echo, a feeling and also a thought, as from some place I'd forgotten, somewhere else. I started to turn my inner-self toward it, to become aware of it. But even as I did it was overtaken by the rush, the excitement, the pleasure of this creature, she, this one with me here in the cool shade. The image of her filled my eyes.

She rolled the fruit up and her teeth vanished into it. The juice spread in a shiny gloss across her lips. I watched her tongue slowly curling, sweeping the traces of juice from the tips of her fingers. She stepped closer, brushing herself against me. Warm, this wonderful creature, this woman. Her finger gone from my lips, she held under my nose the wet lush fruit. She giggled as I sucked the juice and pulp with her, she on one side of the bulb, I on the other. The nectar stung as it spilled into me, a peppery sweetness in my throat, rolling and spreading like heat inside me.

With the strength of an awakened urge, I tasted and felt only energy for her. I knocked the fruit from her hand. It fell with a thud to the ground between us. I felt the dragon staring at me and looked. Its color brightened. It turned and broke, fleeing up the core of the tree, its tail propelling it, slapping the bark as it sped up and away. I looked back at her. I looked at her naked body, her curves against the still, humid air. I looked and said nothing. I only wanted.

"You are looking at me." She jumped around the tree and away from me.

I stepped toward the tree, toward her. "You shouldn't look like you do ... so good, woman. My woman."

I circled fast and grabbed her from the far side of the trunk. With her wrist in my grasp, I looked at her—my desire, my certain delightful desire, my sharp, warm want. I pulled her toward me, her arm straightened and bowed by the force. I held her tight, her breasts flat, pushing myself against her.

"Let me have a look at you," I said.

She kicked at me. I jumped back, still holding her wrist and pulling her with me. Pushing me away with her other hand, she lunged forward, pounding me on the inside of my thigh with her knee. I tried to dodge her blow and slipped, stumbling against the tree, scraping my hip deeply on its bark. I lost my grip and she sprung away toward the trail. She reached it before I could regain my balance.

She glared at me as she struggled onto the horse, a look not only of anger and fear but of clarity, as if the solution to a long-sought riddle had just been made known to her. I put my hand to my side and yanked it away, wet and sticky. The scrape had reddened and in thin stinging slivers, dark blood rose for the first time, a terrible shiny red, flooding my torn skin.

Needling the horse, she turned sharp and hard, nearly causing the beast to collapse. The animal cried and jumped into a gallop. Its hooves dug into and threw a spray of hard, rocky soil.

With the taste of citrus in my mouth, and the noise and dust of her retreat settling round about me, I stood at the tree's edge. In the middle of the path I stood naked and alone.

Oren of Susa: Proof

Several times, with the aid of Mahesh, I have sent messages to Amat. I have told him a fair amount about my time here. I've told him about Adam and this place.

I sat down again nearly one hundred days ago to send him another message. I asked him to do a task for me. I had decided there was something he could do, a way to possibly prove what Adam was telling me. And a way I could stamp out the last bit of my doubt.

I was specific.

Faithful Amat—

Do what I have written here.

Close the tablet house for the necessary days. Gather your traveling bag and make a plan to visit each of the villages opposite Susa. Go to them in this order: Shuruppuk, Unugg, and Ninbru. If you learn nothing in these, close the tablet house for more days and visit Nurim and Anzanuran.

For lodging, go to the scribes in each place, greet them in my name and they will give you a room and food.

While you are in each village, follow the scribe's direction and speak with the market lords and the overseers—the village elders. Ask these rulers if there was a woman named Eve who was known there.

Carefully note what you find. Send me the outcome of your search in a letter from each village. You need only give your letters to the scribes with which you board. They will pass them between themselves until they reach me.

I trust learning the truth of this will be easy and will give some public fact to the story this man, Adam of Eden, is telling.

Send word on the way of the tablet house, as well.

Until then.
Oren

Writing this short letter to Amat reminded me of a conversation I'd had in the village with a shopkeeper. I met a fellow who told me that if Adam and Eve were in fact the first man and woman then everyone descended from them. The shopkeeper pointed at me. "Even you."

I think of this again. If this is true, then this story Adam is telling me is a great family history. These are the sort of stories—many of them, anyhow—a father would tell his children so they can tell their children. My writings of this first couple might be carried far from here, read by those who can read and told to those who can't.

Within a couple of weeks, I begin getting notes back from Amat. The first comes from Shuruppuk. This is clear from the scribe's stamp that Amat had been lent in order to send the note.

Master Oren—

I have begun the travels you asked of me. Indeed, the scribe here in Shuruppuk is hospitable. He became helpful, too, as soon as he heard your name and saw the letter that you sent to me. But I have spoken to the marketers and village leaders. No one here has heard of Eve.

They are bored with my questioning. They've no idea what I'm talking about. I will leave at first light.

Amat

The notes from Amat then begin to come in the intervals of his travel from village to village.

Master Oren—

Unugg is everything Shuruppuk was not ... lovely, covered with vineyards, the smell of baking bread.

The scribe took me to meet the head of the village today. This village elder was intrigued by the story of Adam and Eve. He asked me to repeat it to him and then to several other men whom he brought in later.

They, too, were fascinated.

*When I was all done they told me none of
them had heard of these two before I arrived.*

*I have been hired to carry a collection of
messages to Ninbru, thus I have become a sort of
traveling story teller and letter-carrier.*

Amat

With that, Amat moves on. He writes to me from
Ninbru—the scribe in that town is Amat's older brother
so he enjoys that stop for a few extra days—and Nurim.
Within a day of arriving in Nurim, Amat is told there is
a woman named Eve in the village. But after checking
in on her Amat sees. "She is several years younger than
myself!" The young woman's mother tells Amat that
when she was a child she met an old woman named Eve,
who was passing through the village, and the name had
always sounded beautiful to her.

Amat travels on.

Master Oren—

*I am finally at Anzanuran. I didn't know
villages grew to this size! There are dwellings
here the size of small mountains, and gardens on
roofs!*

*The first village elder I spoke with was very
quick to tell me that simply yes, there was a
woman named Eve.*

*Because of what happened at Nurim I was
not too excited, but then he went on to give me
details.*

She lived in a private walled house with many family members. He told me that she was the first woman and the first mother. She was very old, the oldest of any woman known then or now.

"She is no more" said the elder. "She has been with the spirits for three harvests."

If I may, Master Oren, I think that based on this and what you have sent to me previously, this man must be who he claims. It is not hard to smell a liar, and a madman gives himself up at every turn. Surely this fellow is neither.

Further, since this Adam is who he is, then this Maker cannot be easily denied, can He?

All has been well this season at the tablet house. The boys are attentive when it rains and not so much when the sun shines. The older ones ask after you.

If I may, on the days of no class, I'd like to travel to see you, and this Adam. I'd like to see him again. Please tell me if this is acceptable to you.

Faithful in all.

Amat

Before I left Susa I gave little thought to man's beginnings. If someone had asked me I would have said we cannot know the gods, the ancient gods whose carved images stand upon the poles by the river. Perhaps I would have suggested that they conjured us—perhaps in a contest with one another—have grown tired of the game, and now conspire against us.

Adam's claim of a solitary Maker challenges me. It speaks to me of what I thought I could not know—a God who made man and woman with His own hands, who spoke with them and spent time with them. A God who made all things, a lone God who not only crafted but also cares for man and woman, a God whose carved image is not on display for us but who walked with us? Who made all that we see to remind us of Him?

I want to believe we were created like this, made by a God who knows us. I want to believe this. I want to believe in this one great Maker-God.

Maybe it is this revelation of Adam's God, or the idea that everyone I've ever met must be a relative—that the messenger I met on the road into Susa with the boys must be my cousin—but I need fresh air.

I step out into the nighttime breeze and stand looking across the dark sea. My eye passes over the waves and up into the heavens. I step down onto the beach. I sit and then lie back. I look up. And I see the lights of God.

Chapter Seven

In the Moonlight for Her

As the light of dawn began to put out the stars and pink the sky, I walked back the way we had come. It was too late for insects and too early for birds, the quiet found only at the hour between dark and dawn. The moon remained bright, stretching my shadow and dappling the path. I shivered, chilled by the breeze. Each time I touched my side, I felt the sting of the tree bark. The pain was unlike anything I'd ever felt before.

Each movement in the forest caused me to look. The breeze stirred a patch of ferns; an opossum descended a tree and ran into the brush. Where was she?

Even as I searched for her I felt like I was on display. Every sound I made circled out and echoed back. I feared I might not find her. I feared that I would. And what would happen if I did? I felt like a stranger, a thief in my own land, as if I was skirting the base of a watchtower. I thought of how I might fashion a covering for myself, a cover against the cool air, something between me and all of this.

Rather than being covered in soft dirt and patches of moss, the path was washed out. Rocks like upturned bowls caused my ankles to roll at each step. My back ached with the buckle of my knees. Smaller rocks dug at the bottoms of my feet, threatening to puncture and cut.

How far could she be? She could not be home yet. She could not have ridden that hard, that far.

Morning came. The sun began its climb as if today was only another day. But I knew it was not. Today was different.

For the first time in my life my stomach was empty, holding only a twisting ache. Any other day I would have easily found a meal along the trail, but now I passed caches of vegetables lying on the ground. They were too soft or unripe. Many were covered with a layer of tiny flies. I picked one up and blew the flies off of it. I nibbled at the side of it, and then stopped, gagging and spitting it out as a gray rot oozed into the corner of my mouth. In the middle of the path, just ahead, I saw a bird pulling a worm out of a hole in the ground. Disgust ran through me as its beak held tight and sucked. The worm twisted up around the bird's nostrils and in on itself in a slimy, desperate jig. I gagged again, pitching forward in a heave. Thirst came over me.

I felt like giving up my search. I circled back a short distance, and stopped at one of the pools to rest. Could this be the same pool in which she had bathed? I was sure it was but it had changed, it was altogether different. The water was cloudy; the bottom must have been down there somewhere. I sat on its edge to drink, dangling my feet and legs. Leaning over, I saw a dull outline, a vision of myself on the surface of the water. I looked worn, used up like the half-rotten vegetables on the ground. The skin hung in little sacks under my eyes. The whiskers on my face had grown dry, stiff, and rough to the touch. I reached between my knees and scooped the water. It was luke-warm and tasted of rock. I washed in it anyway. I rubbed my ears and eyes and ran my hands over my hair. As I did, a few hairs fell out, twisted and gray around my fingers. I caught a sniff of the nectar on my hands. A fragrance that was once sweet was now soured and stale like old wine.

Some very small, flying creatures huddled at the edge of the pool. One landed on my arm. I watched it and then felt it as it drove a small thorn into my skin. Once I would have named the creature, but now I slapped at it and watched as it dodged my blows and sailed up into the air, its underside bloated and red.

I stood and continued my search for her. I could see even this far along the hooves of the horse had hit hard. The forest opened up. There were fewer trees. The path ran atop a ridge. Clouds hid the sunlight and I felt sad, empty. I called her name and each time the silence collapsed in around me. In not protecting her I had lost her. I had lost my purpose. A deep loneliness hung over me. It was something well beyond a want, it was a wish. I held inside me, and still do hold inside, a painful wish that I could go back, back to the day before. I could have gone with her and struck that dragon; I could have protected her. But instead I had lost her. Then I had turned on her.

The day wore on. I decided to stop and make a camp with what little solid wood and broad leaves I could find. I started to step off the path and into the trees when I saw, on a rise in the path ahead, our horse, nipping timidly at some clover mixed with thistle. I ran to the beast. It stomped and backed away from me. "Settle, settle," I said.

I bent and looked at the marks on the path leading up to the animal. The horse had jumped to the side, landing hard, hooves together. I stood and looked out into the brush all around me for any evidence of where she might have landed. Undergrowth stood high and thick, many strides deep at the edges of the path. I stood at each side of the trail, searching in the dimming, evening light.

I stood up straight and listened. There was a moan, a muffled human sound. I could not see her.

"Where?" I said, as I spun in a half circle trying to divine the direction of the sound.

"Leave me alone."

It was her. The voice was weak, but hers.

I slid down from the trail and began to push through the thick grasses and barbed vines. Pulling them aside, I moved slowly, hunched down, clearing my way before each step. I heard her again and turned to the side two or three steps. There she was, lying flat on her back. With less care I'd have stepped on her.

She said nothing as I approached and she did not try to move, but stared at me, her eyes wide.

She looked so frightened. What had I done? "I will take care of you," I said.

At first I was not sure she knew I was there. But as I knelt beside her she closed her eyes and slowly opened them again.

"Cover me," she finally said.

Relieved, I searched around us and found some large leaves, not unlike those I had used once as part of a roof. I laid them across her, covering her so all that remained to be seen was her head. I pulled some of the surrounding vines and brush closer against the cooling air. I gathered still more of the leaves and made a pillow and bedding for her, pushing them under and around her, a nest.

She said nothing. I had caused this. I had caused her to needle the horse so that she was thrown. I had submitted myself to my desire and now here I was trying to somehow make everything right again.

I determined to put in a fire and stay, and then push on at first light. The fire smoked, flaring up only now and then. Hard, dry wood was not to be found. Using browned leaves, hollow, brittle briars and some fallen bark, I caused a trio of small flames to push up. I managed to gather a few scraps, some carrot and a few tree nuts, and heat them over the fire to almost warm. I found a couple broken sprigs of sesame and crushed some peppercorn between two rocks. A fleck of these herbs brought some muted flavor. I lifted bits of it to her lips. She ate one bite, then two before her eyes fell shut. I ate a bite and set it aside.

I lay down beside her, among the weeds and between briars, worried and unsure of her, of us, of what would happen to us.

He had told me.

"This tree is not a beginning, it is an ending. To taste of it is to leave all else behind. To taste of it is to die in its shadow."

"Die?" I had asked.

"Life can be taken away," He had said, "replaced with dry stillness. Dust without breath."

"This knowledge brings a death? To taste of it is to know and die?"

My questions were those of a child's, sent up easy and often, not tethered to the weight of experience. In asking, I toyed with ideas and realities that were distant. The questions now sounded like prophecies.

He had taken a step toward me. He wanted to make sure I heard him. "I brought you here, to this tree, to warn you and ask you to leave it as it is."

And then He walked back toward the trail. I had not followed and He had not waited.

How would I tell Him? He would know. He would see. This place was not the place I had known even one day earlier. Food did not rot. We did not bleed. Animals did not eat each other! And I had never looked on my wife, my other one, as if she were a thing to be had. As I lay there I caught her looking at me. She did not smile. Under that tree, in the slimy juice of the rind of citrus I had lost the ability to read what was behind her eyes.

A confused and heavy mind can be forced to slumber, but it takes a great deal of wine, and as I had none, I lost more sleep than I won.

I stirred just before daybreak, startled by the sound of the wind. The tops of the trees leaned and pitched, yet the stars were bright, clustered and pulsing, visible here and there beyond the swaying canopy. The grass and brush swirled as if in a fit.

She was gone.

As I jumped up, the ash from the fire caught a gust and pushed a cloud around me and up across the path. I choked. My eyes burned and teared as I stepped deeper into the woods, hoping to burrow up under some low growth or stumble into the mouth of a cave. The horse had moved only a little further down the path. I could see only its head, raised and motionless, listening.

"Stay there and be still." Her voice came from the dark behind me. "He's coming."

Turning and staring into the dark, I barely had time to understand what she was saying when I heard my name.

"Adam?" His tone was searching, seeking. The wind grew still.

I felt sick; heat rose into my face. A dread came over me ... a drive to hide.

"Adam. Where are you?"

Too much had occurred in the last day or two for me to be prepared to see Him. I looked back for her. She made no show or sound. I fell to my knees and crouched, frozen to the turf like a hare.

"Where are you?" More urgently this time, asking the air where I was.

I looked in the moonlight for her, while He looked for me.

I pushed myself deeper into the grass, I felt a fluttering in my chest and I inhaled the scent of dirt. My own waters flooded the earth beneath me, creating a mud that pasted itself onto my groin.

As I lay with my chin against stems and roots, He came into view through the brush. At first when I saw Him I stared, stunned. Was His skin hanging from him in folds and layers? Then I realized He was wearing a pale-green cloth that appeared to be one piece, wrapped around His entire body. He moved a few steps at a time up the path, scanning the forest. When He got to the horse it shuffled its feet toward Him, holding one hoof up from the ground. I lifted my head a bit higher and watched as He stroked the beast, lifting its hind leg and tending to the hoof. He bent and seemed to breathe on it and cover it with His hand. He then patted the animal softly. It turned and skipped away, down the path.

Hoofbeats gave way to silence.

The Maker stood still, listening, watching. He did not call again. I did not know if I was hiding or if He was letting me hide. But I was sure it could not last. I knew who He was. I was hiding in a place He had made. If He wished, He could order all the animals to haul me out before Him. I lay there anyway, knowing He wanted to find me. And I knew what He wanted, He always got.

My neck and shoulders were numb from peering up, but still I stayed and watched. And so did He. He stared right at me, or what felt like right at me. He couldn't possibly see me through all of these plants, could He? I was trapped, there was nothing I could do but lie still, there in that very spot. What parts of me weren't numb were aching down to the bone. After a while, knowing I was trapped became the reason to end it, the reason to move. I gave up.

Slowly, through pain and tingling, I pushed myself up onto my hands and knees, pulled myself forward, found the edge of the path, and crawled into the middle of it.

Revealed in the dawn, I stood myself up, my knees and back stiff and crackling. I turned to face Him. Bits of grass and grit stuck to my thorn-pricked belly, elbows, and thighs. He must have seen the silver sheen of ash coating my back and legs. My hip bore the ugly crusted lines of blood from the scrape of the tree.

He looked me over in silence while I began to try to find the story. I thought about how I'd lost her, or how she'd left me. Which should it be? It had been her idea to go to the tree.

He came closer, until He stood just a pace away. Every impulse was to retreat back into hiding, to scamper back to my burrow. He looked at me. His eyes looked up and down my body as if looking to see how damaged I was. He then leaned in and put a hand on each of my shoulders and pulled me toward Him. He wrapped Himself around me. I shook as I sobbed. Regret came in waves. And I knew ... I knew then it was surely gone. I knew that what I had always known of this place and what I had been, that perfect first man, His greatest wonder, was gone. He held me as I cried, as I wept until I was weak, and still.

I lifted my head. His shoulder was slick with my sweat and tears. And as words formed I felt the turn in who I was, in whom I had become, the brokenness around me, through me. I felt there was she and there was me in this moment. And the words fell from my lips against His ear.

"It was she. If she had not been so insistent—"

But as I lifted my eyes to His face, I saw that He was looking down the path. His attention was not on me.

I turned to see her, this lonely observer, standing in the morning sun. His arms dropped from around my shoulders, and He pulled away from me, giving no indication that He heard me and He stepped toward her, holding His hands out to her.

An invitation to join us, I thought. I reasoned that she should come, take her part of the blame and some of the hope I believed He could offer us. She moved her gaze from Him to me. Had she somehow heard me, heard the blame I had laid on her? A thick stew of pride, anger, desire, and disgust bubbled inside me. A bruise on her cheek and another deeper, larger one edging up her thigh and onto her hip made her look like she had been beaten.

She looked again at Him and backed away two, maybe three steps, her feet moving toe to heel in the dust. The Maker paused, not moving any closer, treating her like a frightened doe. I thought she would be reckless not to take what He could offer. Even as I thought this, I did not know exactly what that would be.

"There you are," I started.

"You will not call to me." Her cold tone matched her unwavering stare.

He took a step forward. She looked at Him.

"I am right here," He said.

Her knees began to shake as she let out a cry and fell to the ground, limp. Her hair scattered, covering her face. The Maker ran up to her and bent down. Kneeling, He lifted her, gathering her, carefully tucking each arm into His hold. Her legs draped over His elbow as He picked her up. Mud fell from the bottoms of her feet.

I stood watching the two of them. This time, they were so different than the last time they had been together before me. Then He had been presenting her to me, her new and perfect hand in His. Now He was rescuing her from me, stepping in to catch her as she fell.

Without words I took the lead as He carried her home.

Oren of Susa: A Past Together

Adam sits across from me still and quiet, looking out the window. I set my lap desk on the floor beside me and reach for my tumbler of water. It appears we are done for the day.

"As you told me about Eve being thrown," I say, "I was concerned—"

"Liana?" says Adam.

Telling Adam about her has laid bare an old wound. Why did it happen to me, to her, and what could I have done? Until I told him, I hadn't told anyone about Liana in well over half my lifetime. But as I told the story I found she has not faded. She has not aged.

The moments on that field are like a rich and horrible drama. I look and there is the quilted, grass-stained fringe of her dress. I hear the men's voices as they gather around her, their torches turning the dusk scene to a sickly daylight as they elbow the young actor, playing me, out of the way.

I watch and it is real. And one of the men says what I already know, that Liana is broken and she feels nothing. And all the men turn toward me. Not toward the actor playing me, but toward me, sitting in my seat. And all the village of Susa has been watching the play with me. And the action stops. And they all turn toward me. But I have only regret, guilt, and loss, like a pile of glowing embers in my gut. They can't see these. They wait and eventually, one by one they turn away from me back toward the stage. Her father and mother are the last to turn away, seeing I have no lines.

Perhaps this is what Adam sees each day as he tells me his story—the action of it relived, played out in his memory before him. But he had Eve. He had her by his side.

"You didn't have to go through what I did," I say.

"But what if?" Adam picks up the thought. "That is what I asked myself for a long time after, what if something worse than bruises had happened to Eve?"

"You wonder if The Maker would have replaced her?" I ask.

"Or would that have been possible?"

"The Maker didn't do it for me." The thought comes and I say it—a bitter and brutal fact I'm just now considering, that washes over me. "He didn't replace Liana. I've had to try to do that myself, or live without her."

"I'm sorry," says Adam.

We sit. There is the silence again, the silence that comes of looking backward into time, of studying the past closely.

"When you were hiding," I ask, "was The Maker letting you hide or were you hidden from Him?"

"I don't know. I, too, have wondered that. The more I've thought about it the more I think He was letting us hide."

"Then, as you crawled out of the brush and stood before Him, could He see your guilt?" I ask because I wonder. I wonder if He can see mine—hidden away in that space I've made for it, under my cloak, above my belly and at the base of my heart, the glowing embers still hold their heat.

"He is The Maker, Oren. He sees. He can feel all creation, seen and unseen, the past and the present. I think He knows each place where what He has made has been broken. He knows what has come, and what will come, of our not leaving it as it was. And He relieves us of what we give to Him."

"You are so sure."

"Once I was new to guilt. Mine was the first guilt. And like you, I learned to hold my regrets and my failings like hardened objects, stowing and silencing them. With what we do and what we say we've become very skilled at cooking this stew. But The Maker can relieve us of it all."

Adam tells me he once turned his guilt over and over, turned it so many times it became like a smooth rock in his hand. "We are speaking of my Maker, my Father," says Adam. "I know nothing else. I give you what I know."

And I let myself imagine it—opening my cloak and my pain to The Maker. I imagine The Maker peering into the darkness of my core and seeing the orange glow of what has defined me. I am out of hiding. And The Maker offers to take the embers from me. To take what has been my curse and my comfort.

And I place the embers, one by one into His hand.

Chapter Eight

East, and in as Many Days

The grains, flowers, and vines of home looked as if they were without a keeper. Some had given up and fallen over; others had been picked clean by birds and were matted down, covered by droppings. These plants I had tended with my own hand now looked as if they were making their last stand against the ugly plants around them, wrestling with them in a last effort to maintain their place. My sheep in their matted wool gathered at the fence and cried to us as we passed, their lambs huddled under them trying to nurse. As we neared, I looked over at the trees. Under every one of them lay dozens of pieces of fruit, fallen, split open, browned by the air. A bee I'd never seen buzzed each piece while tiny worms drilled holes in them. Clouds cloaked the sun, the sky a sheet of gray. The lack of sunlight hid all color.

I pushed open the door to our house and held it as He entered. Passing in, He turned sideways to keep from bumping her head or feet, careful, as if what He was holding was the most precious plunder, now rescued and being returned home.

Kneeling again, He laid her in bed while I stood in the doorway. I peered in a couple of times, peeking, knowing there was nothing I could do but wanting to anyway. I had offered many times to carry her as we walked home. I had stopped and turned, and held out my arms as if to take her. He paused and shifted her up in His grasp, the sweat running down His face, and looked at me for a moment, only long enough to lift His head in a quick jerk telling me to keep moving.

When He was done He came out of the room and passed me without a word. I followed Him.

As soon as we were outside He turned and looked at me.

"She begged me to see it for herself," I said. "The tree of knowledge was all she spoke of."

"So?" He waited.

"Over and over ... she wouldn't give up."

My argument sounded thin even as I said it.

"You knew though, didn't you?"

I knew. Yes, I knew going back was a mistake. I'd given in to her. "I knew I wanted peace."

"You had peace. Her asking you to see the tree, asking you to take her to see it, that was peace." He looked away from me toward the lamb's fold.

I heard her call. I turned and ran in, leaving Him standing alone in the yard. But she hadn't called. She was still in bed, just as He'd left her, wrapped tightly in weavings which had once been only wall coverings, intended as decoration.

I paused at the end of the bed, her feet nearest me. Her breathing was heavy. She was asleep, on her side, her head turned away from me. I settled in next to her and sat up in the bed. I put my hand on her back. She did not move. I leaned over and looked at her. My lover's eyes looked dark, the bones around them like the edges of shadowed pits, the bruise on her cheek like a grass stain. But this was only the part of her pain that had surfaced. What of her pain could I not see? What of her pain might she never speak?

I awoke the next morning in a heap next to her. An early crow called, making that sound that had once taught me its name.

Kneeling in a shallow corner, submerged to my neck, I sat still, drinking my third tumbler of wine. She moved slowly, deliberate and graceful. Her cupped hand pulled water in tiny waves over her shoulders, each stroke creating a whirlpool which vanished as it reached her collarbone and the shadow under her chin. We bathed ourselves, she on one end of our favorite pool and I on the other. She looked across at me. I could see that she had tried to hide the last of the bruise, somehow blending its green hue toward her brown.

We had been home for seven days and our routine had started to find us again. We cooked together, even though what we found to cook had little taste or was overripe. Everything was half of what it had been before. The green of the leaves, the spices, the milk and eggs, all of it had lost texture and taste. The delight of it had drained away.

It was as if our mouths were numb. Taste fell far short of memory. She still had her way; she did her best work with the goods we collected. We didn't go hungry.

The beauty of the place was dulled. We saw the land as if we were looking through haze. Colors were muted. The air stood still with odors instead of wafting with scents. The rich smell of loam was too often overrun by the stink of some rot.

And there was a tension, a space between us, which I was sure we both felt. Our thoughts were only shared in words, and these had become much scarcer between us. I had once heard a speech in one of her looks; now I questioned my ability to have the first knowledge of what she was thinking.

The work was tangled in change as well. Ugliness was injected into beauty. I held sheep while she used a sharp flint to cut away the snarls in their wool. We helped the newborn lambs latch onto their mother's teats. Those that wouldn't suckle were lost. They died during the night, but we never found their bodies. At the base of the gate we only found tufts of wool. Had we dropped some of the shavings? No, for ground into the muddy wool was dark-red blood. The wool had not been cut; it had been torn, ripped from their flesh in clods! What sort of beast could do this? What beast would take another in weakness? I thought of the worm and the bird and wondered if the larger animals were pouncing upon these helpless ones and taking them in their teeth. I didn't want to think about it. The idea was horrible. Such possibilities worked at me, at us, and added to the unease between us.

I took an entire day and walked the orchard, picking up all the bad fruit and tossing it in a pile at the edge of the forest. I wanted to talk to her about what had happened, but finding words was harder than when we'd first met each other, that moment in the garden when He had presented her to me.

She stood at the edge of the pool with her side toward me. Water ran down her back, breaking just above her hip and rolled the full length of her leg. Wet, almost black, her hair hung to the front in thick strands over her breasts, the ends curling a bit more with each drip. I stood and walked, the water at my waist and then at my knees. Her thin ankles and glistening feet left shallow prints in the mud, the dip of a heel hanging below a crescent arch looked upon by five perfect ovals. I laid my heavy, deep print next to hers. She still moved me.

She paused and sat on a rock at the base of the path back up to the house. I stepped around her and found another spot to sit as she smoothed bellflower oil on her arms and shoulders. I felt like I could burst. The need to talk to her was physical. She was all I had. The need was nearly pushing words out of me, but what to say?

Several days earlier I had finished making the garments, coverings for both of us out of leaves of flax.

I did this because she had kept herself wrapped up in the tapestry, the wall decoration He'd put over her, ever since we'd arrived home. She walked around bundled up like she was in a cocoon. If we'd talked about nothing else, we had talked about that.

"I feel like the trees and the animals are staring at me. The air wraps itself around me. You look at me too."

"No I don't."

"Yes you do, when I am naked. My breasts hang as I cook. I have no privacy."

"What do you mean, privacy?"

"I mean when I am bare it is uncomfortable. I don't feel safe. I get cold. There is nothing separating me from everything else. Can't you understand?"

All I knew was that I was not as physically fine as I had once been, the hair on my chest was losing its color and when I sat a bulge formed at my middle, rolling onto my thighs. She didn't say anything about my body, but I knew. And yes, I got cold sometimes, but I also didn't want to always be covered up, bound up, especially when I was working.

But I made our shells; I made coverings for us using the material of the decaying land around us. As I made these coverings I felt we were melding with it, like we were now making ourselves a part of it, blending in with this broken place. I imagined if He looked for us now we would go unseen in the land, covered in dry brown plants.

I made my covering so that it covered only my hips, groin, and rump. I also made a gown, but I didn't wear it often. The coverings felt awkward and rubbed at me when I walked. Strips of wool on the inside made them comfortable enough to wear. "Good. I don't want to look up and see you always naked, like an ape," she said.

I made her covering so that it covered all of her, from her neck to her ankles but she had me trim it off so that most of her arms and legs showed. Her legs became the part of her body that I most admired. I'd never fully seen the shape of her legs and the beauty in her arms.

Using oils and "covering up," as she started to call it, became an entire routine. Being covered gave us each room for secrets and under these our selves began to take form. She began to have emotions that I could not understand, moments of tearfulness, even laughing while crying. And there were long periods where I did not speak but made myself busy in the garden. She complained at my lack of words. "Why don't you tell me what you are thinking?" Indeed, under these coverings I became he and she became she.

As we began the walk home I determined we must speak. We couldn't be silent toward each other forever. I began to look ahead up the path toward the house, picking out spots in the trail where I could say my first words, and then we'd pass the spots in silence.

Finally I quit thinking and let go. "The bruise ... it is better."

"I saw my reflection in the cooking pot this morning," she said. "It is fading but I still put the darker oil on it. And I dusted it a bit with pollen."

"You did well," I said.

This was more than she had said to me in days and days. Much more.

"I want to tell you." I paused. I was twisted up inside. I wanted to tell her I was sorry, but I wanted to hear her say it instead. "I wish I could go back and keep you from that dragon."

"I have never felt this before," she said. She was herself. Always clear, to the core. "I have never felt this hollow want. I wish things were the way they were before."

"I shouldn't have taken you there," I said.

"I think we're different in ways we don't know. I think He looks at us differently too."

"I'm sorry I wasn't under that tree with you sooner," I said.

She stopped walking and turned, we faced each other. "What would you have done?" she asked.

It was a good question. What would I have done? Stare and watch? Would I have grabbed the dragon by its tail and slung it spinning end over end into the bushes? Would I have picked her up and run from under the tree, galloped away, my heart pounding at our escape? I didn't know, but I was sure this wouldn't have happened if I'd been under there. The thought brought little comfort.

"I would have told the dragon what The Maker said," I said.

She looked at me. "I did. I told the dragon what you told me; most of it anyway. It seemed to already know."

"But it didn't," I heard my voice grow louder by a tick or two. "It was not there. It couldn't have known."

She said nothing.

"Didn't you wonder when it spoke? Other than the angel, I've never heard a creature speak."

"No. There was a sense in the moment. It was the place. It had an 'other place' sort of feeling under there."

I knew what she meant by that. It had felt like anything could happen under that tree. There was a cool other-world under the shade of those leaves.

She went on, "I was playing with it. I was stroking it. I held my hand in front of its mouth and it stuck out its tongue and tickled my fingertip. I thought it was a gift from The Maker. I thought it lived there in the tree. It spoke so kindly; it said so much to me. There was a life behind its eyes."

She began to walk again.

"I saw you and my desire for you turned demanding," I said. "I want you to know that I would never try to take you like that."

Her eyes rose and she looked at me. "You were not you."

"I know," I said, "but it was me who frightened you under the tree. I don't ever want to be fear to you."

She did something that I could never have imagined. She stopped on the trail, turned, and kissed me. It was not a long kiss, but it grew from the same passion that her kisses had so long ago.

"Let's find again a place where we can be together always," she said. "Let's try over again."

I took her hand and looked into her eyes. She pulled at the shoulders of my covering and it dropped to the ground. I lifted hers from off of her. And we saw that we were not only naked but bare, we stood before each other unhidden. I felt my face flush with worry, with shame, fear that it might be too much for her. To have me so near. The oil had made her skin soft and the sun warmed her. A bed of soft moss grew at the side of the trail. She took my hand and lay back upon it. I bent over her. She pulled me down, her arms tight around my back. We were still, for these few moments, one.

"Yes, we'll find that place," I said. "You and I."

I was glad that He had given us some time to be alone together. We'd had time to learn to make our way in this bent and crippled place.

To one side of the house were several lower fields, pastures in which I kept a variety of grazers. They gave us milk. I was also beginning to gather clean wool and find uses for it. One of these lots, the smallest of them, had a flock of new lambs, most not more than a season old. One evening we walked the path which opened up on these grounds. She was the first to notice Him among the lambs. He was sitting down among them as if tending them, but He was looking at them, closely.

"Keep your eyes straight ahead," I told her in a hush.

There was no point in attracting attention. He was far enough from us and the path cut up an incline, away, toward the house and the orchard beyond.

"Let's walk faster," she said.

I put my arm out to hold her back. "But not too fast. We will draw His eye."

He did not look up before we were out of sight.

She slowed and turned to me. "What was He doing?"

I shrugged. "Looking at the lambs. I don't know."

"I know He was looking at the lambs, but He wasn't looking at them, He was looking at their bodies like He'd never seen one before. He made them!"

She was right. I shook my head. There was a time when I felt I knew and understood His every move. Now, I was more comfortable without Him. It was easier. Just she and I.

The house pitched a long shadow across us as we returned. It felt good to be inside. Safe. We had woven thin strands of moss with grass and covered the windows and doors, letting in some light while keeping the insects out. She lit a wick and began to cook potatoes, garlic, and pepper. We agreed that bedding down early would suit us. The days brought with them a weariness that seemed never to fully lift. Sleep no longer came quickly and stayed. Sometimes we would lie awake and wait for the spinning of our thoughts, the sunken past and burden for the future, to slow and allow us to drift off. The days were long and difficult, spent finding food and keeping our home protected. We began to think of inside and outside. We began to concern ourselves with animals that might come in and take food we had collected for ourselves.

As she cooked, I stood at the front window, looking at nothing, still lost in wondering what He was doing down there. Here He came again, strolling up the same way we had come. He walked straight and tall as He carried one of the lambs draped over His shoulders.

"Look at this," I whispered.

She stepped over beside me. "Where is He going? What is He doing?"

He passed near the corner of the house and continued around the wine press, along the orchard and out of sight.

"Should we go see what He is doing?" she asked.

I hesitated. My desire was to avoid Him altogether and simply stay in the house. "Yes, I suppose. Let's go see, but let's not linger with Him too long."

She nodded and we walked back outside in the direction He had gone.

Stacked fieldstones had been formed in a short square pedestal. On the top of this some brush smoldered, starting to catch, and push a thin stream of smoke up between the tree limbs. Leaves fluttered at the end of their branches, spinning on their stems from the heat. The lamb nibbled the leaves off a shrub nearby.

The Maker did not look up as we neared. He spoke to a small beast He had trapped under His foot. He bent over, grasped the creature, pinching it between his forefinger and thumb, and stood. I did not recognize the creature until its eyes caught mine.

I saw a stripe of blue scales running from its snout to the tip of its tail. And I was back there again. I was under the tree with her. The citrus was in her hand and the taste of it was numbing the tip of my tongue. The fruit was falling from her grasp, hitting the ground and rolling between our feet, and the dragon was staring at me.

The Maker held the creature so that we could get a good look. I looked at her. She gave nothing away, no hint that she had any recognition at all. How did she do that? She had washed all emotion out of her face. But I kept looking at her, and as when storm clouds are pushed down into a valley, I saw behind her eyes gathering shadows of fear.

The Maker turned to her. "Why did you listen to this beast?"

She looked at Him and then at me.

"It spoke so well ..." Her words trailed off and she looked at the ground.

As I looked at her I remembered how she seemed to have been entranced under the tree, how I had had to go under to get her.

"It is true," He replied. "The dragon does speak well. His words come twisted and turned with an ancient ease."

He now turned to me. I didn't need a question. At the edge of this fire, with the dragon looking on, in this moment He had constructed, I fell away. I slid back into my ways, back into my easy ways of leaving her on her own, of abandoning us. I did not resist myself.

"My thoughts were not with me," I murmured. "I was led along." And after I said it I began the familiar tracing and retracing of blame. I believed this was true, didn't I? There, under the tree, hadn't I been taken off my feet?

The beast wrapped its tail tight around His wrist and twisted its neck against the tip of His thumb. It wrapped so tight it turned His hand red and opened its mouth halfway as if to bite. The Maker held the dragon close and spit on its tail. The beast's tail uncoiled and fell limp, hanging, swinging in midair. He spoke to the creature.

"I have given you your days of roaming free, but you will not walk away from this. You have chosen the dust as your bed. You will look upon the hooves of all other beasts."

He placed the creature on the ground and pushed his thumb down hard on the top of its head, the beast's jaw pinned shut. "The dust is now your bed; the powder of the earth will cake your chin and coat the corners of your mouth. You and the woman are enemies, as will be your and her offspring forever. Her Child will crush your head as you strike His heel."

Lifting His thumb, the creature's tail quickened again and began to move in a new way, side to side, its legs hanging limp, shriveled, and useless. Into the grass it vanished, it's back slithering in the dirt like its tail. It left behind a track like a rope dragged behind a horse. I saw her move away, her shoulders pulled up tight in hatred of the snake.

The Maker began to gather more firewood, so we did too. As we all bent, gathering fallen wood and vines, I wondered what He was doing with such a fire. Couldn't we cook and eat at the house? Or I could simply have brought some wood from the house down here with me.

"I could go get some wood," I said to The Maker and to her. "Maybe, if I can find any, I could gather some fruits, some potatoes or cabbages?"

Neither of them was listening. She stopped and turned to Him. "What was it you said ... 'her child'? What does this mean? Will there be more of us?" she asked.

The Maker looked up and smiled. "Many more. You will see your numbers grow until you cannot count them or name them all."

She looked at me. I looked back at her. "He's never told me any of this."

"Yes." He stepped over and took the firewood that she had gathered. "There will be more of you, but life will begin and end in pain. I wish it were not so."

"Why?" I asked. "If You wish it were not so, then make it not so!"

He spoke to us both. "Because of the tree. You did not leave it as it was. Because of this eating, all I created has changed. The comfort and ease of this place is gone."

The lamb bleated, shuffling its hooves in the grass.

"What else?" she asked. "What else is changed?"

"Life will bring moments of joy but long hours of struggle as well. You will try to make your husband your own but he will demand much of you."

She looked at me. I knew what she was thinking. She had already seen this. My demands of her. She wanted to be close to me and I left her standing alone when there was blame, when there were difficult questions.

The Maker turned to me. I thought that what He had said was enough. Too much. What else could there be? "And the earth will demand much of you, Adam. Work will mean loss of enjoyment."

I looked down at the wood in my arms and the blood trickling from my thumb. There was a tree I had never seen before that had thorns. While He was talking to her one of the thorns from this tree had slid up under my thumbnail.

"Work," He continued, "hard work will now be the way you feed yourselves as well as the way you will prosper. You will no longer simply gather fruit that hangs in clusters all around you. Life will be only work for you. The soil will produce for you, but only because you force it to, only because you sweat over it. You will work the dust for a lifetime and then you will die. Dust again."

The Maker walked to the edge of the stand of trees and faced in the direction of the sun's rise.

"The next seven nights are to be your last in this birthland. You will begin to make a plan for your travel east, and in as many days you will do so."

Protests rose in my throat, though I knew they were futile. "Why? Why should we leave our home?"

"You must go from here, fill the earth, be fruitful and multiply, subdue it but also tend it and rule over all creatures. In other places you will live out your days, far from here."

"But I began in this place. This is all I've known. It is all we've known!"

He went on to promise provision in our leaving, further welfare for our descent into this unknown and adverse life that was to be ours.

"You must go from this place, but my hopes for you are great. In you I have made all mankind."

"You have hope?" I blurted in disbelief. "Hope for us?"

"Yes," He said, "for your future and for those after you."

I thought of those who would come after us. Their origins would be asked of us. There were parts of this story that would be hard to tell, difficult to unravel. There were secrets I wished to be tucked away in the folds of our skin, like a vine wrapped tight around a maturing cedar. There was going to be a child, more than one. I could not imagine a child or a herd of them, but He'd said it: too many to count. Lives would come from her, only from her.

She is the mother of all living, I thought. "Eve."

She looked at me. "I will call you Eve. I am Adam and you are Eve."

"Adam and Eve," she repeated, giving it meaning.

The Maker gathered the lamb into His arms. I thought for a moment He might ask me to take it back to its flock. But He didn't. He held it tightly.

It whined a little, but didn't squirm. Fire nipped at the leaves overhead.

Oren of Susa: Of All Things

I ask Adam if he has seen The Maker since Eden. No, he hasn't, but he feels His presence all the time. "It isn't only that I think He's watching me—us, Oren—though I do. It is more than that. His efforts linger here in what He has done, and I know He is still sustainer of it all."

"Do you think you will ever see Him again?" I ask.

"He said He would be back, be seeing us again."

I pause. I don't think I'm ready yet to tell Adam about my experience of several days before. I can't be sure I'll ever tell him.

I traveled north one afternoon. I had never been that direction and had decided to explore further up the coast from Adam's home. After walking for a couple of hours I came into a small town at the edge of the sea. I don't remember the name of it. As I walked up the beach I could hear the sound of music and many voices. Several children ran past me. Wagons were parked all along the road outside the open gate. Once inside I turned a corner and it was clear that all the people from the village and the countryside around were in the streets. It was a festival or celebration of some kind—troupes of dancers, performers with wild animals in cages, and pits with great fish roasting on spits. Beer and rice mead were being pulled from the largest clay jars I'd ever seen.

I did not know what they were celebrating. I wandered down the street, weaving around or between one small group after another, through the crowd. I had walked deep into the fair, when I saw him.

He was in the middle of the crowd. He was muscular and tall; his face was cut like sculpture. He had long black hair and no beard. He was lovely and moved with such grace and ease. One crowd of admirers after another gathered around the youthful-looking man. Some hugged him while others reached out and simply touched him. He picked up children and held them, kissing their cheeks.

The thought came over me that I was watching an event—one for which I'd been prepared.

I stood perfectly still and watched as several revelers offered him toasts and songs. Like all the others, I felt drawn to him. I must approach him, I thought. I made my way up, another small crowd dispersing with much fanfare as I approached.

I stood before the man and said nothing. I wanted to hear his voice. I wondered if he would know me, having seen me all these days—so many moons spent sitting with Adam in his room at the end of the hall, writing the story. I waited for him to smile, perhaps say my name and suggest we move away from the crowd as he knew I had many questions. But within only a few seconds I saw that the man was looking to me, waiting for me to say something.

"Are you Him?" I asked.

"Am I who?"

"Are you Him ... The Maker?"

The music started again and grew loud behind us. The crowd formed into a tremendous set of circles, one inside the other, four deep, and was beginning to move like a great spinning dial, one in the opposite direction of the next.

"Did you say, The Maker?" asked the man.

"Indeed, The Maker!"

"The Maker of what?"

The music grew yet louder. I spoke in an awkward yell. "Of all things—The Maker of all creation!"

"Of what?" The man looked at me and leaned forward.

"Of all things!"

"That is certainly the first time I've been asked that!" The young man looked at me smiling. He had a puzzled look, and said something else—his lips moving and his head nodding. I couldn't hear him. A gap came in the music. "I am glad you are enjoying the drink, my friend," he said, winking at me.

I'd missed part of what he said. I started to ask him to repeat himself, to tell him the noise was too much, but he turned and moved into the center of the most inner circle of dancers. I looked after him, unsure if he'd answered me or not. The circles began to move faster as I stepped away, back toward the side of the street.

Just then I saw, walking toward me, a furniture maker I once knew well. He had lived for many years in Susa. I turned to him, surprised to see him—a familiar face in this strange village. I wanted to explain what I thought was happening, who I thought this young man must be, but how could I tell him all that I knew? All that Adam had told me and how I'd come here and—

"Why hello, Naman," I called.

"Oren, my old friend, I saw that you met my son."

"Your son?" The dancers seemed to be turning me as well. "Why the last time I saw him he was only—" I felt off balance, trying to piece it all together. "Yes, we've been chatting a bit."

"Well good! Indeed he was no taller than a new calf when you last saw him. How fortunate that you should see him again ... and on his wedding day! I wasn't expecting you, but how good that you are here!"

I told Naman it had been too long and we should make a point of reuniting sometime, although at that moment all I could think of was what Naman would think when his son told him of the conversation he'd had with me.

As soon as Naman clapped me on the back and wandered off to greet other guests I turned and found my way, skirting the dancers, back to the edge of the feast. I grabbed half a chicken, a tumbler of drink, and left.

Chapter Nine

Somehow and Someday Turn

I hadn't fully understood what He was doing, though I was unnerved and alarmed by the lamb's bleating and the crackling fire. But when I saw the sliver of sharpened flint and the way He held the lamb in the orange light, it became clear. I leapt forward, grabbing at His arm, pulling in urgent attempts to move His hand back and make space between the knife of flint and the yearling's throat. My tugging was like that of a child's. I hung on His arm as the lamb's eyes went wide; its knees locked straight, and its hooves stamped into the earth.

I released my grasp on His arm as the blood of the lamb sprang in an arc and fell down my leg, flowing, a dark red and then purple as it mingled with the dust and pooled in soft, flat bubbles at my feet. I pulled my legs under me, struggling to regain my footing. I was shocked at how very much blood there was. I panicked and bent forward, screamed at Him, "No, no! Wait!" attempting to undo the damage. In those moments, which slowed as all such moments do, I fell to my knees in the dirt and cupped my hands under the stream of warm, wet blood. I began to collect it so I could somehow return it to the limp and gasping creature. But the blood ran between my fingers. I bent down and began to gather it from the ground. I scraped at the pooling blood with my hands. I cried and then wept for it all to stop. I held my reddened, soaked hands up, cupped as tightly as I could toward the lamb's throat and looked to see where I might funnel the blood back in, back into the silent, struggling creature.

He held the lamb's head tight against His thigh as it quit the fight, its soft white wool now pink from its chin to its forehooves. Its final cry came in a weak gurgle as its eyes rolled hard to one side as if looking up to me for hope. At this I spun away.

Just as quickly as I had thrown myself into this scene, I now exited it, gagging then retching, the firelight making the trees and vines appear to flicker and jump around us.

I forced my head to lift and I looked at Eve. She appeared to be fighting the urge to turn and run. I watched as tears flooded the beautiful creases at the sides of her nose and fell from her chin, glinting in the firelight, picking up speed as they tumbled down and vanished into the thin rivulets of blood that had turned her dirty feet into islands.

This yearling that had playfully bumped heads with the other lambs had been no different than the one whose soft jaw I had cupped in my hand, its delicate pant tickling my inner wrist as it waited for me, its protector, to provide its name. This yearling now lay a few yards away, lungs emptied, teeth bared.

The violence had ceased, but the results of it caused us to shiver. The split it had created within our memories would last the rest of our lives.

We huddled together as The Maker went step-by-step about his work. There was no sense of hurry. He moved with confidence, with thought and mastery, each turn and the next step following a plan, a process. The way of doing this had been set, prepared for us. This act created for this moment caused me to wonder again, as if for the first time, who is this Maker?

The lamb lay just in front of the altar, in a heap, stripped of its skin. He bent over it, breaking no bones, cutting when He could, tearing when the job demanded. He showed strong emotion. His face was tight, even as tears ran down. He didn't look up or around. He didn't slow or hurry. It was clear that each step was being done for us. The drama was in fact a series of skills to be learned for future use. He was teaching. Teaching me not only the art of butchery, but how my nudity might be relieved, how some semblance of reality should be pieced back together, how grace should be obtained.

He stood straight now, each piece set out before him. A bed of large leaves, fig and palm, laid under them. Then flawless, smooth muscles were dropped, one-by-one onto the fire. This was not done fast or as if He was throwing the slain lamb away. Pausing after each piece, He would look into the heavens and raise His hands as if to attract attention to what He was doing. As the body of the lamb sizzled and darkened, I was amazed to find that an aroma filled the air, a sweet and robust smell came from the cooking flesh.

He motioned us near to Him. We did not come. We stood back, frightened, causing Him to ask us again. His apron stuck to His bare chest, soaked. His hair hung wet with sweat that continued to roll down His face as if He had been working in the fields since dawn. We stood behind Him as He turned to face the altar and knelt, speaking, not to us, but in tones of request. "And for these, Father, I give this one."

With His words came calm and a respite over the entire scene. Instead of the heat of a brutal slaying, the place took on serenity. He tore the meat and gave it to us to eat. So we did. We took and ate. It was foreign, like an extra tongue in my mouth. And so it was that we took this death within us while His presence brought us a hope. Hope that what had happened, these last nights and days together, would somehow and someday turn to a sort of good again.

Before, sleep had come quickly, seducing deeply and staying long. It was now only seen slipping through the edges of our nights, a once intimate friend turned stranger.

The eighth morning we were up early. The rising sun chased away the darkness as Eve took a few last items and arranged them into bundles on either side of our horses. It was a very cool morning. The dew on the grass chilled and bit my ankles, causing the hair on my arms to rear up. The morning insects had multiplied. They hung in clouds and some nibbled at us causing us to itch. Pink streaks appeared all up and down our legs as we clawed at ourselves.

As I waited for her to finish, I wandered over to the altar and held my hand just above the ash, piled up like scoops of gravel. The stone basin was still warm from last night's sacrifice. Drops of dried blood splattered the base. The sacrifices had become my task. I had prepared the lambs and built the fires every evening at dusk. Eve would stand with me, but for both of us, this never became routine. While the point of it was purity for her and me, a making right of that which we had made wrong, the act of it was a filthy business. The lamb's blood, the spilling of it day after day, had stained my palms a blush pink, the same color as their skinless, drained and drying muscles, the same color as my cheeks and neck as I worked. My gut emptied each time: I had to force my mind to focus beyond my response and seek that peace that came as I lifted my eyes, turned my face upward, and raised our requests for forgiveness. But seeking forgiveness was a skill I would fail to turn into a practice.

I turned toward the house to see if she was ready and saw that she was standing near the horses, looking off toward the orchard. She was looking at The Maker.

He came toward us carrying two cloaks. They appeared to be made of some sort of heavy brown leaf. But as He got closer, we saw. They were made of the skins of animals. Over these past nights He had come and taken the skins of the sacrifices that I had cast off and had made these cloaks to cover us.

"Come here," He said, "each of you, alone."

She went first. She walked up to Him. He took hold of the covering I'd made for her and tore it down the back, peeling it off of her. There she stood, naked in front of Him. He lifted the skin covering He had made and set it on her shoulders. He wrapped it around her, tying it in the front. He then pulled her to Himself and wrapped His arms around her as He kissed her on the forehead.

It was now my turn. I stepped forward and stood before Him. He looked at me. I looked into the same face I'd seen that very first morning, under the tree. The look in His eyes was one of pure love. He had made this place, this entire world for me. I was His son, His heir.

He reached down and tore the covering from my hips and dropped it to the ground. I too now stood before Him naked as He lifted the cloak of animal skin and hung it across my back, dressing me just as He had dressed her.

The coverings I had made lay tossed to the ground. Their leaves had long ago turned brown, their edges thin and feather-worn. I had tried to cover our bodies, to hide us from each other and from Him. My coverings had been made from what I had at hand, a pale attempt to correct what only The Maker could. Only He could make coverings that would cover us, only He could patch His creation.

He had covered us, covered our nakedness. With this He had done all He could for us. The coverings He had made for us from the skins of sheep and goats were good. They were welcome warmth and protection. They had come of bloodshed. This was the way He had chosen and crafted for us. At first they were strange against our skin, but in time they became a part of us and a reminder of who we were, that we were at risk of being unprotected, uncovered. I feared they were a sign of the difficulty to come.

Where He had gone was, as always, something of a mystery. He had a home that He suggested I would see one day, but today felt like a step in the wrong direction. Leaving makes coming so distant. This place was home. All I knew had originated from the turf on which I now stood for the last time. I had always traveled with the knowledge or at least the expectation that I would return. There had never been this imposed finality in my departure, this being pushed out and away. The length and depth of my travels had always been to accomplish a task; however, even those trips were not to be anything permanent. Thus, leaving home was what we were doing. There had been no uncertainty in His words and there had been none in His tone.

"As you leave, which you must, this place will no longer be a sanctuary for you," He said. "Go, care for the ground and see all I have given you. East. Go to the sea. Its provisions are many."

"Sea?"

"Sea." He scratched the language in the dirt. "It is a great water. A watery, salted crater that preserves life."

"Unlike our rivers?"

"Without flow. Like a lake but much, much greater. With ebb that pulls and pushes, feeds and balances the rivers."

A giant salty and shifting lake? I decided to ask no further. We would ride into the rising sun.

All was ready. My dog was ready to follow along behind us. His jowls had turned silver-white and he didn't run as much as he once had. I helped Eve onto her horse's back. She sat nearly at eye level with the edge of the roof of the house as she looked down at me. I handed up to her a special covering I had made for her for the trip. She held it, looking it over and then looking at me. I gestured, laying my hand on the top of my head. She looked up at its wide brim which shadowed her dark eyes.

"What made you think of such a thing?" she asked.

"I saw a tree-cat settle under hosta leaves to gain shade from the hot sun. It gave me the idea."

"And now I'll find the shade too, as we ride," she said.

"I call it a head-hat."

"I feel safe under it. Really. I am so surprised!" A smile filled her face and then just as quickly it fled. Made of vine and woven grass from around our home, the hat would serve as a keep for her memories.

From the back of my horse I looked across the yard. The orchard was in bud and would soon begin to push tiny fruits out to an absent keeper. Several barrels of last year's wine would wait forever in the corner of the winepress, save the barrel strapped to my horse's hind. We had started a small fire and baked some herb cakes that morning, so the chimney seeped its last bit of smoke.

Putting my head down, I pushed my heels into the sides of the beast and we left.

She may have looked back. I did not. It was enough to see my few lambs left in their pen at the base of the hill. I had left the gate open. One of them called as we passed off into the forest. Its echo fell into the brush behind us.

When the sun was fully up, we crossed the final river valley and climbed before cresting a peak which would be the last in the birth land. I stopped and climbed off my horse. Walking over to an outcrop of rock, I looked across the fading green hills and stood for a moment. This was the border of what I had known. Beyond this we would be gone.

From here I could see one of the rivers as it trailed off into the lowlands. Eve stepped up behind me, standing close. A herd of oxen or some such bovine, I couldn't remember which and it didn't matter, amassed itself at the base of a hill, near the river's edge. Clouds hung in bright white puffs over the entire scene, creating drifting shadows over the river grasses, foothills, and plains beyond. It was larger and greater, a more delightful land than I would ever know again.

We began our descent into a place and future. There was a promise of provision. There was also the promise of pain, and the fact that we were to be dust once again. I looked back up from where we had come. There at the highest point, looking after us, a creature stood in the center of the path back into Eden.

I paused and turned. When my horse, saw the creature, it backed slightly in a nervous prance. Eve had not seen it yet, but stopped too. She turned her horse just in front of me to follow my gaze. When she did see it, she gasped.

With the shape of a man, the creature stood, saying nothing, motionless but breathing. It returned our stare, demanding not fear but honor and respect. It filled the space where we had passed just moments before. I had not heard or seen it come. At least twice my height, or more, it had a mane of feathers across the top of its head.

"It's an angel," I said. I pointed to the skin of its arms and face. "It has skin like dried milk."

The angel wore a wrap of clothing that looked like scales and its face and manner were set with the ability to seal off our return into the land. In one hand the angel held the curved horn of a beast, but this was a longer and wider horn than I had ever seen. The angel lifted the horn to its mouth and blew. From the horn came a call, vibrating the air, shaking every leaf. In the other hand it clutched a hard-looking blade that reflected the sun. As the sound faded it lifted the blade in notice of us. A goodbye.

And so it ended. Close we had been to The Maker. Not only close, but with. We would now rely on His past words to us and our memories. He had said He would not lose track of us. We had told Him, too, that we would be careful to not be hard to find should He come seeking us.

I signaled to Eve that we should start again. She looked over at me and pulled her horse close. She leaned over and put her hand on mine. We sat together for our last few moments in Eden, saying nothing. With all my faults, she was casting her lot in with mine. She was leaving behind all that had happened and was going with me. She hadn't begged to stay behind with Him. She was content in who we were, in who we had become. Would that I could have been the same.

I pulled ahead and led her, my wife, my lover and my helper, into a new life of which I knew nothing.

And somewhere ahead lay a thing called a sea.

Oren of Susa: Sea Bath

It is early morning, just after breakfast. We've not yet started writing for the day. Walking down from the house I see no one. Standing alone on the beach I look one way and then the other. The vacant shore stretches on in either direction. The air is warm. The sun has lightened the sky but has not yet broken over the horizon.

I will try the sea.

I strip off my smock and lay it across a log of dried wood that has rolled up onto the beach. Stepping down into the cool water, just up to my ankles, I feel the sand at the bottoms of my feet.

At home in Susa I bathe in the river where the bottom has been made hard by generations of feet pounding and the current sliding endlessly over it. Bathing in the river, there is new water constantly moving around and past me and the temperature of the water that comes and goes is always the same.

Neither of these is true of the sea that now laps at my knees.

191

I have seen the sea every day since my arrival here at Adam's house but I've never bathed in it. The one time Adam invited me I refused. But now here I am. And the water has a sort of softness, a fizz that bubbles up from the sand. I feel cold and warm mingling around me. This water is rising and falling against me, a sliding and shifting mass. It seems I could float in it like a plug of tree bark.

As I wade further in I start to notice odd rocks at the bottom. Some feel pointed and others smooth. I bend to pick one up and see that it is not a rock but a wonderful figure, like a carving. I pick more from the bottom. Some are like bowls and others are like tiny pillars. I jump and shiver, startled as from one of them soft fleshy parts reach out and prod my palms. I fling these back into the water. Most are empty but all are colorful. I walk, feeling along with my toes. My knees buckle as I bob down into the water and reach for them.

I splash handfuls of water onto my face and lean back, soaking my head and floating in this flood of creation. "What is that salty taste?" I say aloud to myself, using my tongue to collect and spit the water from my lips.

And I realize it is the water itself—"salt water" as Adam calls it. And he is right. "How very salty it really is." I say again, "Terribly salty!"

As I wade a little deeper, the salty, ebbing water pulls at my feet. It is like a river under the sea. I feel the power of it. I churn my arms at the surface and jump, pulling myself across the waves toward the shore.

I sit on the log next to my smock on the beach and let the sun dry me. A soft white dust is left on my skin as the sun does its work. I brush at it with my fingertip. I touch my finger to my tongue. The salt.

I have swum in the sea. A grown man, I've been for an hour like an exploring child left alone to bob at the edge of a great puddle.

And the sea is a wonderful thing to me. Its constant energy and movement—the greatness of The Maker felt all around me. I will fill a jar with sea and take it back with me to Susa.

Chapter Ten

To Hope, but When

For the first time in our lives we were without trees, without shade. We watched the towering foliage of Eden shrink behind us. With each step it grew smaller until it was a knob on the horizon. We stopped and turned for the last time, and it was gone. I held my hand up over my brow and felt a loss, a loss of a here and there. Panic rose in me, a fear that every way was the same. The sun rose and the sun set, that was all that marked this place. Upon my horse I was the tallest thing I could see in any direction. I was on the edge of the land, exposed. I could be plucked from the ground by one of the flying creatures by day or hit by a falling star by night. My neck and shoulders cramped and ached from hunching forward, away from the hovering sky. All the sun's power bore down on us; the glare of its full light caused our eyes to drop and squeeze nearly shut. We were in the land. We owned the land. But we were without a home, we had no place.

All that was not sky was brown. Light-brown or dark-brown or some brown in between. There were green sprigs of plant now and again, a very few had grown, turning and knotted skyward until they were as tall as my horse, but even these were leaning toward brown. Each step found us where no man or woman had ever been. The land was made of rock and dust, an expanse that was flat, plain, and dying under the great dome of sky. I wondered if this place we were traversing was what remained, what was left over, the scraps of land after He had made Eden. I wondered, too, if it had always been this way. Had this place changed like so much else and become like this when we were under the tree?

We rode our horses all day the first day, all night, and most of the second day, stopping in the late afternoon in the mouth of a cave. We put in a poor fire using bits of stalk and a few shriveled chunks of wood I had hoarded from among the rocks. We ate a dried fish I had taken from Eden.

The sun was still up as I knelt to lie down next to Eve. I wanted only sleep. She had just begun to lay down when she cried out. "It hurts!" She sat straight back upright, holding her legs and arms at slightly bent angles. I started to ask what was hurting, but as soon as I bent my knees the pain came as if my skin were tearing, splitting. "What is it?" My voice echoed into the cave and back out. I was now frozen in place, afraid to move at all. There was nothing touching us, nothing I could see!

Eve finally, bit by bit lay back very still, saying nothing. I put my hand on her arm. "Your skin—it is red, and very warm." Her legs and arms had taken on a deep red hue. I had ridden, almost since we'd left, with my back exposed to the air.

"Yours too," she said. My back and neck felt like they had hot ash spread upon them. My legs felt like they were hanging over a fire. With much groaning and what little aid we could give each other we stripped off our garments and lay naked on the cold flat rock of the cave floor and tried to sleep through the shiver and sting. What had happened to us? Would this pain be stuck to us forever?

The next morning we found that water bubbles had formed like puddles, trapped just under our skin. With these came fatigue, an exhaustion that kept us from any traveling. We lay in the mouth of the cave, rising only to eat a few berries we found close by. After some days, our skin cooled. Then it itched. It itched as much as it had burned. We did nothing but drink water that we found in the cave and scratch each other. While she slept I stood and slid my back up and down against the wall of the cave, against the black crust of the rock with such force that I thought I might shave the skin from my shoulders. In the end we were lifting thin dry leaves of skin off of each other under which soft new skin was showing through in patches. We made a stack of the dry skin at the mouth of the cave. Eve made a grim game of it. "A layer of mine, a layer of yours, a layer of mine, of yours, mine, yours ..."

We knew the sun much better now.

By the new moon, as the land descended into the darkness of nighttime, it would take on a bitter cold. During the day the heat would build. There was sometimes relief, when a breeze would push in and cool us. But too often these breezes became winds, sometimes great gusts stirring up into dark clouds we could see approaching, great storms of dirt. Stinging sand and dust drove us to take cover. All we could do was slip between a pair of rocks in a low spot and wait.

Eden had held us close, the sun, shade, and breeze constant. But here we felt like weevils on the face of a sunflower. We were traversing a desolate land. We were tossed in the wind. A day's walk felt like we'd gone nowhere. I thought of the trees far more than I had in Eden. I dreamed of them at night. I wished for even just one. I asked The Maker, I uttered into the air, "One tree." And He heard me. That evening, we found one; a lone one, thin and weak. It was not a sapling but instead was old and stunted. From its base to its tip it was but a head taller than my horse. I could wrap one hand around its trunk. But it was a tree. We stopped and sat under it for several days. We felt its bark and stroked its leaves.

We continued to walk into every sunrise and away from every sunset looking for the sea.

With our traveling there was no time for planting or harvesting. I am not sure I could have made anything grow in among the rocks and the few spindly plants that were already there. Perhaps a plant would have taken hold, but it would not have been in the ground very long before it had been scorched by the sun.

It was odd, too, that the animals ran from us. They seemed threatened by our presence. Maybe it was because we were so different? I couldn't tell. No matter how soft or with what call I tried to approach them, they would turn and run, go into a hole, or take flight. Before, before the eating under the tree, the animals would approach us, or at the very least they would stand and look at us. From the panther to the bat, they would interact with us, live with us.

My understanding of the way the animals behaved in this new world was nearly formed, but it was not until one evening that I truly understood the last of it.

While walking and picking grains, I saw ahead of me a bear on an outcrop of rock. I called to the creature. It looked at me and rose up on its paws before coming down to a crouching position. I continued to call to it, talking to it, saying its name.

As I came closer it leapt from the rock and landed on the path ahead of me. I called again to it and again the bear lifted itself up and dropped back into a crouch. As I came to it I stopped. I reached out to it. It sat up, with a low and warm rumbling sound, only its back feet on the ground. I spoke its name once more. With great speed it lashed out, swiping one of its paws and catching me in the forearm. Its claws punctured and pulled the skin and a layer of the muscle of my arm into ribbons. I jumped back and cried out. The bear jumped forward and burst forth with a roar, its mouth in a vicious yawn. Foul odor like a fog rolled from between its parted jowls. I surprised myself with my reaction as I kicked, yelled, and finally screamed at it. The bear turned and ran, nearly straight up the outcrop of rock, over and out of sight.

I found that the wine was a salve to my torn arm and enough of it caused sleep when none could be found. Eve wrapped my arm in wet leaves from a small tree, the only one in sight, and packed clay around it. For many days we ate only a few grains that she gathered and a couple of nuts, from that same tree.

"If I could go back ..." I heard myself say, the wine bubbling in the pot of my gut.

"What would you do?" she asked.

"I would have moved us. I would have moved us as far from that tree of fruit as possible. Of all that was in the land, that one tree—"

There was nothing left to say. My arm throbbed.

If that was the way it was to be, then I would alter myself toward the animals as well. Fierceness was inside me too.

I had at last, after thousands of tries, become very accurate at throwing a rock. I had thrown rocks in Eden, only for fun or to fetch a piece of fruit that was out of reach. As I've said, in Eden the rocks were lovely, colorful wonders. Here they were all the same color. Gray. They were not polished or rounded. They were jagged and edged. This made them ugly, but it also made them easy to grip for the purpose of throwing. I had learned how these new rocks would fly, even how they would bounce. I had learned I could skim them off other, larger rocks, off boulders if I needed to.

My first hunt and kill was a ferret.

The ferret was standing, tall, settled on its back feet with its front legs drawn up. It was facing away from me. I had somehow managed to sneak up so it did not hear me.

I was eight gallops from it, not close, but with it showing itself to me like this, distance was less important.

I had set out before dawn. I was carrying several rocks in a satchel I had made during the first few days as we traveled, sewn from the stomach and sinew of a dead goat we had found. I stood still and reached in without taking my eyes off the ferret. My hand rested on one of the flat, thick rocks, one about the size of the palm of my hand, perhaps only a little smaller. I lifted the rock out and in the same motion with the other hand I raised the satchel from around my neck and let it slide down my leg, slow and without sound, to the ground.

While learning to throw rocks, I had also learned to always stop prowling in a stance, in such a way that my feet were in position, ready to throw.

Feeling the rock in my hand, I stared at the ferret so as to aim. I stared at the back of the thin beast's neck. As I did so I was amazed to hear the creature hissing in alarm while its back remained to me. It was then that I saw it; a manul had the ferret close, frozen under its watch. This was terrific, utterly in my favor! The manul was focused on the ferret and took no notice of me. If I took the ferret, the cat would run in alarm from the action. And the ferret was distracted, open to my hit.

There was a part of me that filled with grief to think in these terms, to allow my empty stomach to rule me. I had named this creature, this one whose neck I now studied in order to split it. But Eve was sitting miles behind me under a rock ledge with a piece of unripe and dried-up fruit she had found, just as hungry as me, awaiting my return. I was learning that life was to be much about doing what I did not want to do.

The cat was hunched and would at any moment spring on the ferret. I lifted the rock over my shoulder, looking only at the neck. I let all else fall to the sides of my vision. The neck loomed larger and larger in my eye.

In one motion I shifted my weight to my back leg, kept my front planted to receive my follow-through, and pulled the rock forward at a great speed, as if throwing my very hand into that neck. Just as I came around with my arm, the cat sprung too. But a manul, even at full sprint is not as fast as a thrown disc of sharp rock. I watched as my rock caused the ferret to drop several strides in front of the cat. The cat jumped in alarm, straight up and over the ferret. It was a success!

I ran as fast as I could over the rough terrain and up to the ferret. With pride and sickness I looked to see that my rock had nearly sliced the ferret's head from its body, the neck was laid wide open in the sunlight.

I picked up the ferret and used another rock to fully remove the head. I rolled the skin down over the body of the animal to reveal a dark red, sweet-scented meat. A bit of wine and a cooking fire were in order. Perhaps a few grains could be found here and there on my way back, to bed the meat.

The same scent I remembered from the first fire He had made in Eden traveled in one small stream of smoke from the fire that evening.

"What is it called?" Eve asked.

"Ferret."

"Are we to have meat without a sacrifice?"

"We are hungry and this is His provision."

I gave her a hind leg from the small fire and settled back with the other.

In order to feed the two of us I had learned to take animals. I had learned how to hunt them, how to seek them out, become one of them and prowl. While ferret would never become a favorite, that night we were soon full enough and I was drowsy from the wine. We slept through the night and into the next midday.

This was the relationship we had with the land. Everything was ours for the taking, through the work of our hands and heads, just as He had said. We trudged on toward the sea. We stopped every ten or twelve days and built a crude house where we would stay for a couple of nights—sometimes longer.

These homes reminded me of the shacks I had built in the naming years. I structured these homes out of stones and grass, long grass that grew in tufts among the rock and had begun to become more common as we went. These homes were free-standing structures with dirt floors. A couple of times we laid rock on the floor too. We cooked just outside these homes, as we could, for it was constant work collecting bits of wood or stalks of any plant that might create heat. I found that I could dig a deep narrow hole and line it with rocks, sand, and clay in which to keep water that rose from under the ground. I made one of these for us and one for the horses. The horses had learned to nibble at whatever greenery they could find. The tall grass was a welcome sight for all of us. Any tender new growth was taken by them on sight. Like us the horses were not fat but they weren't starved either. We were all adjusting. I was doing what was necessary to find food, while she was making a home for us, part of which moved with us as we went. With the woven mats she had made and the bowls of palm bark we had found, her horse soon had more strapped to him than when we'd left Eden.

We sat outside one of these homes by the cooking fire one evening. I had taken another tumbler of wine although what we'd brought with us was nearly gone.

All our talk was of food, making camps, and the past. Tonight, as always, she started with the question we couldn't answer, the question that always led us nowhere.

"Why did He put that tree in the land?"

I turned and looked at her. I loved her. I wanted to answer her questions but I had no idea. "He wanted to see if we would leave it alone."

He had given us a choice. I felt the guilt rising up in me again, the regret like an old familiar cud. These were the feelings I most often had when it came to our relationship so I said what I'd said a thousand times. I said what I always said when we talked about this, or about anything in Eden.

"I should never have taken you there. I should have done more."

"What Adam? What could you have done?" She was trying to help me recover. She still loved me too.

"I should have cut it down."

"Could you have done that?"

I knew that I couldn't. It would have been like burrowing through a mountain.

"I should have tried."

204

The sea was nowhere to be found. We traveled east, stopping and setting up our little camps when we could go no further. We stopped one sunrise for a rest after traveling three days and nights. As Eve came down off her horse she cried out. I ran over to her to find that her foot had turned on its edge and had slid between two rocks. Her ankle was caught fast in the crevice. Taking a smaller rock I began digging to try to dislodge the rocks that held her. It was two hours before the rocks began to shift at all. I kept below her, clawing at the dirt around the rocks. The dirt was hard like baked clay. She sat on my back, trying to take the pressure off her trapped ankle and I kept below her, digging, digging. I dug until the mid-day sun was shining down on us. Only then was I able to slide the rocks apart enough to lift her swollen foot from between them.

I set up our camp in that spot and we stayed for many days. Her ankle became the size of a knee and then two knees, soft and bloated. I worried she would be lame. I wondered if I should cut her ankle open to let the blood out of it. I imagined carrying her now and forever. Perhaps we could find a stout goat that she would use as a support when we were not traveling. She could use that goat until it died and then we'd find another.

But the ankle became itself in time, although it bothered her the rest of her days.

We had traveled many moons and the land had changed. The tall grass was plentiful and a stream of water could be found here and there. Trees began to appear, nearly full-grown trees. I thought again about the thing called a sea. Where was it? Had we missed it? That seemed impossible. Was it covered by this grass that was growing forever around us?

I was delighted one day to spot a vine. It was a tiny one, with its tender broad leaves and curly stems. I dug it up, with patience and care, just as I'd unearthed her ankle. I kept it damp and tucked away from the wind and sun so that I could plant it at one of our stops. No, at our last stop. At our home. I imagined plucking grapes from it, and from a hundred more vines grown from its seed. I imagined crushing those grapes and making tumblers of wine, a tumbler for every evening, forevermore.

With the grass came herds of roaming beasts, some with horns. Some were great runners. We would come over a hill and there would be a herd of grass-deer. They would see us and shift, a thousand of them in one movement, and run like a flock in flight, across the expanse and out of view.

My thoughts tumbled back across all the land that was between us and Eden. Back to Him saying how He had hope for us, and what our future held. It was hard to hope, but when we arrived at the sea I would sacrifice a dove to Him. I determined in my soul that He would hear me. Also when we arrived I would take the outerskin off of Eve. She would lay back at the edge of the sea. I would remove my covering and lie next to her and say the word "love" to her. And after a while she would roll over toward me and hold herself up, her arms straight, hovering over me. With her staring down at me, her hair lifting on the breeze, dark waves framed by the sky, I would rub the small of her back, my fingertips up and down her spine.

But for now I lay with the vine tucked close, under the cloak of animal skin. The last of our wine warm in my belly, I lay with my head in her lap. In the wilderness, in the shadow of a tree I slept.

We stopped our horses mid-stride. We had traveled for seven hundred moons, in the open land, rock and dirt giving way to shallow rises and bowls, tall grasses in sandy soil pulled back and forth in the wind.

We had come over a rise in the mid-day sun, expecting more of the same. But now before us, as far as we could see, lay what looked like a great mass of the sky had fallen upon the face of the land.

"Is this the sea?" she asked.

Was it rock, a crystal slab of blue rock? I had never imagined water so vast that I could not see across it. The nearest edges bumped up over the land and kicked the rocks, washing the shore in push after push. It was as if the land had melted and pooled under the blazing sky.

"I think it must be," I said.

"Is this the end of our journey?" she asked.

I thought for a moment. It had not yet occurred to me that it might now be over.

"Yes. I will build a final home for us here," I said.

I would build a home again, like the one we'd had in Eden. I could make it all again. But I would start by planting the vine in the breeze of the sea.

Then I would build an altar.

She was standing with me, close, her arms wrapped around me. "A place to begin again," she said.

Oren of Susa: Skin

Adam is ill. He shuffles when he walks, which is not often lately. He naps every midday, something I've not seen him ever do before. He has told me that while there is not far to go in the telling of his story, there is more to be told—more he must say. But I fear I will outlast him. And I think he does too. I think He and I share the unspoken fear he will decline further into this sickness and take the rest of his story with him. It is hard to resist the urge to push him along in the telling. To rush.

It was just over a week ago at dinner. There were several of us around the table and a conversation began about Mauna, a group of men in the local village who have created a secret society that seeks to destroy any belief in The Maker. Adam became upset and demanded we stop honoring such men by giving them our conversation. He stood to speak or perhaps to step away from the table when he bent forward in a convulsion. Blood ran down his chin and he collapsed onto the floor. He coughed and gasped. Blood splattered the servants who jumped to his aid.

He was given oils and herbs that evening by a man who is trained in such things. It is said to be his stomach. Since that evening he has been in his room. I've moved my work to his bedside. He eats very little.

A heavy fog has rolled in this evening, the sort that comes at dusk, quiets everything, and stays until very late, until everyone is deep asleep—the sort of fog that precedes a clear, bright morning. Adam is sitting up in his bed, drinking warm water mixed with sea salt. I look around the room, observing how it is put together. Candlelight reveals the thin shadows of the marks in the timber where axes were once wielded against it. I see the round holes in the floor where the corner posts are set.

"Is this the home you built when you left Eve?"

Adam responds softly. His eyes closed. "No. I've always lived by the sea, but this is my third house. The house I built and went to when I left Eve is south of here. Both that home and the first one with Eve were built with what I knew then. This home was built by a fellow near here who makes his livelihood building and knows many things that I've never learned."

I move my chair closer to his bed.

"And Eden was to the west of here?"

"Yes. Eden was far to the west of here. Southwest. I will draw you a map sometime."

For the first time I think about Eden being a real and actual place—a location over the horizon from us, under the same, now set, sun.

"I assume it would be possible to travel back to Eden. Have you ever considered going back?"

"I've never had the desire. It would be too much in the way of memories, I think. And a long, long trip. I am done traveling such distances."

I think of traveling to Eden, perhaps with a cadre of men. The young man in me imagines a great adventure of searching it out. Perhaps the angel is still standing there with its sword. Would we recognize Eden when we arrive in it?

"Do you know if anyone has ever tried to go and find it?"

"No, but surely someone has. There are people who have talked about it. They claim they know someone who went back and tried to find it or came to the edge of it. Such reports are always vague. I would imagine it looks the same as the land around it by now. Perhaps people are living in it and don't even know it. I am sure seeing it would be disappointing."

"Do you ever miss it?"

"Miss what exactly?"

"Eden ... or the life you had there."

Adam considers the question, far away in silence. "I miss it, yes. I miss it very much, like one misses a childhood village I suppose. A place where everything is a wonder at first, is a discovery, and then becomes forever part of home. I miss afternoons and evenings with The Maker, the animals always near, food and wine like none since. Our senses are so deadened, Oren, so muted now. I miss being at the center of creation. I miss things, the trusted things. All that could have never changed."

"So yes, you miss it."

"But Oren, it is not simply the place. The place is set in a time, in a time in which I was once set. It is not a question of whether I could go back, but rather what of the place is left in me. Our places become part of who we are."

"Then it is not so much the place as the time?"

"It is both. I could go and get in the place, go stand in it, but without the days and nights of the time it would be small in comparison, even destructive to the memory. Time and place are so linked as to be one in the same." Adam rolls over and squats at the side of his bed and then stands unsteadily. "Are you tired?"

I jump up to help him, afraid he'll fall.

"A bit," I say, "but not ready to sleep just yet."

"Good." He turns slowly away from me and walks— one step after another, like a child who has just learned— out of the room while calling back to me. "I have something for you. Stay there."

Maybe he is going to draw me a map of Eden and the land between here and there.

I sit back down and listen to the sea against the shore. I wish very much that Eve were not gone. I would ask her about all of this. I imagine she is sitting here with us. I turn to her and I stop short as I notice at the bottom hem of her gown her one ankle is turned inward.

"What memories do you have, Eve, of the trip from Eden to the sea?"

She looks over at me. Both age and youth are held in her at once as she lifts her eyes to meet mine. One eye is like that of a child's, bright and dialed in on me as if gathering light for the first time. The other is a pure, white glaze—all the color drained from it—like the underside of a fish's scale. She smiles at me as if I am finally speaking with the one of them who really knows what happened.

"Leaving. That is all." She stares. "Ask a more interesting question, Oren of Susa.

"The way Adam spoke to me in the moonlight at the edge of the pool and the way the beautiful little dragon spoke to me in the shadow of the tree were not so different. Both uttered words carved up, cooked, and served only for me. Neither said clearly what really was.

"But I was not tricked, Oren. I saw and I took. It was my harvest. I would have done it with them or alone. And so would have you.

"And as I sped away in the dawn light I knew. I was alone for the first time, and I immediately ached with the memory of the way The Maker had held my hand as we walked to meet Adam. No one has touched me like that since."

The vision dissolves as Adam returns. He is carrying something over his arm. "Here, Oren, I want you to have this."

I stand up and step toward him. He holds out what looks to me like a heavy coat. It is not until I grasp it that I realize it is a skin.

It is made of several skins. It has strange and foreign green stitching straight up the back, two pieces laid together and stitched with a very thick wiry vine. The coat is heavy, I assume according to its purpose, with a soft fur on the inside and thick—of the highest quality I've ever seen—aged, soft white wool on the outside.

"It is jack-hare on the inside," says Adam, "and forest lamb on the outside. I added the jack-hare later." Adam holds the coat out in front of me. "This is the coat that The Maker made for me from the first sacrifices after we hid from Him. The coat he covered me with as we left Eden."

I take the coat from him. I hold the heavy garment and look again at the stitching—each stitch—The Maker sewed this together!

"I can't take this. Surely you must wish to keep it. It must mean so much to you."

"It means a great deal, but you know this more than anyone else. I've been telling you what it means all along. I want you to take it. Here." He motions for me to hand him the coat.

He steps around behind me and holds it open. I put my arms through the openings and down the sleeves which, I am amazed to find, come just past my wrists and cup the backs of my hands perfectly. The coat feels like it was made for me. The weight of it lies across my back. The bottom edge hangs at mid-thigh. This first clothing, this covering, it carries all that Adam has told me, his entire story has settled into the nap of these dense, thick pelts.

And I know this is the gift of a man who can see the end approaching.

"It fits you," says Adam with a lift in his voice. He lays a hand to my elbow turning me around and back again. "It fits you. You and I have the same shoulders."

Chapter Eleven

Part Her and Part Me

She told me that her blood, which always came on the new moon, had not come twice now and that she was unable to eat without her food later erupting and appearing again before her. I gave her cornflower oil to drink and she slept long hours.

Her strength had left her. Her face was pale, the color drained out. I thought this was her end, but I didn't talk about that with her.

I didn't know what death would look like, but her body was fighting the life we tried to give it. I wondered how The Maker could say there would be more of us and then take her from me. I grew angry thinking He had sent us away from Eden, forced us on such a journey, and allowed us to make a home at this sea, all while planning to leave me alone.

One evening she came to me as I was sitting at the edge of the sea. I jumped up, surprised she was on her feet and had walked down to the shore.

"You're up. Where did you find the strength to come out here?"

"Look." She shrugged off her cloak and stood naked in front of me, between me and the sea. She turned to the side so that I was looking at the length of her arm and leg.

"Look at what?" I said.

She stood with her palm resting on her middle. "Here." She moved her hand up and down. "It is a bulge. It was not like this even a few days ago."

I knelt in front of her and moved my hand back and forth on the smooth skin of her belly. Indeed, it was pushed out, only slightly, but pushed out.

"I know where my strength has gone," she said as I felt the bulge again.

"Is it gathering in your middle?"

"No, you dull man, there is a child. A child has stolen my blood and my strength."

"A child? You think you are swelling like the sheep and horses do?"

"Yes. I think there is a child growing inside of me."

"One of us? But how?"

"I think it is from us, from you and me. I think that when you have entered into me this has made a child."

I stood and looked at her.

"How do you know that?"

"I felt it. I felt a twinge, a tickle deep inside. I thought nothing of it at the time but now ... I know it was a sign."

I stared at the bulge. Is this what happened with the animals?

"But now I know," she said.

"What do we do now?" I asked.

"We wait. We wait until the child comes out of me."

I remembered His words. "There will be more of you, but life will begin and end in pain."

"When will that happen? When will the child come out?"

"I don't know." She didn't seem to be hiding anything she knew.

"Maybe at the new moon or maybe at the one after that?" I asked.

"Perhaps. It could be then."

She bent down and picked up her cloak. I watched her walk back up toward the house, weaving up the stone path I had laid from the beach. I stood at the edge of the sea and looked at the water lapping at my feet, each wave breaking over my toes. Each moment, wave after wave, the child was growing. Forming inside of her. I couldn't imagine what this must look like, but each moment meant more. We were not just she and I. There was another of us. Another life.

And so we watched. We watched her middle grow.

Each day I drew the arc of her belly in the sand. I drew it high up, near where the grass began to grow, where the water wouldn't wash it away. Lines like slices of fruit; I dragged the end of the stick through the sand day after day and then laid it at the foot of the path. I wondered each time if I'd take it up the next day and draw again or if the child would come.

The bulge grew, larger and larger and we waited. We waited for the child to come out. Days and days. The lines became curves, like deep bowls stacked down the beach. She and I walked in the sand, the length of the marks I'd made.

We boiled seawater and made weak soups of mint and seaweed. Whatever she could eat and keep. We did little else. We only waited for the child.

The wind blew cold and then warm again.

She no longer fastened her cloak around the bulge. She fastened her cloak down to the top of it and then again under it. The mound of her belly showed all the time. The skin stretched tight. It was always warm to the touch.

"I can't imagine what the child will look like," she mused one afternoon as we cleaned a pair of lungfish, wrapping them in palm leaves to cook.

I couldn't either. "Like us, only shrunken?" I thought again of the animals but I'd never seen a belly extend like this and breasts and thighs swell.

"Perhaps," she said, "but very young. Bright and clean like the lambs."

"Yes, soft and lovely in the sunlight."

I remember thinking that surely the baby would have a face that was no larger than the palm of my hand. It would have stiff, dark hair all over its body that would fall off after a few days. I had seen this in elephants and monkeys.

I harvested the sunflowers, grapes, and our first crop of pomegranates. And we waited. I made the season's batch of wine. And we waited.

One night we sat out on the beach after our meal and wine. I was lying back, dozing. "Did you see that?" she asked.

I opened my eyes. "What is it?" I looked all around us, up and down the shore in the day's last light and out at the sea. I looked up into the sky.

"No. Here! Watch my middle,"

I leaned over and hovered above the bulge. I watched. Nothing, then, "There!" I jumped to my knees.

The skin of her middle rolled and sank, as if the child were ready to burst out. I put my hand over the bulge and felt the child roll again, against my palm.

"Lie back!" I said. I took our blanket and crouched next to her. I was ready. As soon as the child tore out of her I would throw the blanket over it so it would not run off. The child poked her again from the inside. It appeared as if bones were pushing up at us, bones and edges.

And then it stopped. There was nothing. The bulge settled back into place. Stillness.

We both stared. The sound of the waves marked time.

"Is it still alive?" she asked.

"It tried to break out," I said.

She began to cry. "But it couldn't."

I lifted Eve in the crook of my arm and held her. I laid the blanket over her. "Maybe it will try again. Maybe it is just resting from its effort."

But I didn't know. And in my voice I could hear that I didn't know and that I thought maybe it wouldn't try again.

"It is a sign," she said.

And that night she came to believe the child was dead and began to mourn at dawn.

For days she drank only hot water and ate plain raw grains. I got her to eat some bits of fish. She mourned until the second night of the next moon.

This was when we both knew the child was quite alive.

I came in late from pruning the vineyard and found her in bed, soaking in sweat and naked, a puddle of water under her. Her legs were wet and shiny, trembling in the dull light of the wick. She said the pain was as if a knot of flesh was being torn from her core. She squatted in the center of the bed and then rolled onto her side. She wept and cried out.

I gathered the blanket just as I had before, but this time my hands were shaking. I helped her lie back and then I straddled her, holding the blanket high over my head. I felt an awareness come over me, as if my eyes had grown and taken over my whole head. Every flicker of the wick, every twitch she made caused me to jump.

I remembered the words of The Maker. "There will be more of you, but life will begin and end in pain." His eyes fell. "I wish it were not so."

"Why?" I had asked. There was a time when I knew Him well enough to say such things. "If You wish it were not so, then make it not so!"

"Because of the tree. You did not leave it as it was. Because of this eating, all I created has changed. The comfort and ease of this place is gone."

She cried out again, fulfilling the prophecy.

I was ready. I would tackle the child the moment it

split her open and jumped from within, even as it ran up and over her for the doorway.

The next time she bellowed in pain was so loud that I cried out and threw the blanket over her entire body, even her head.

"No!" I heard her from under the blanket. "Between my thighs ... I feel it!"

I yanked the blanket off of her and scrambled down onto my elbows between her parted legs.

I sat up slowly, staring. "The head ... its head is coming out of you!"

"Well its body is sure to follow! Help it!"

Of course! The child was coming from under her. I had seen it in the goats and sheep. But seeing the child roll inside her, under the skin of her belly, I had thought ... but now it was coming. There was a thin neck and the round of its shoulders. Leaning forward, using me as a grip, Eve cried out once more, pulling her knees to her chin. Now there were arms and soon a tiny bottom was visible and then the entire child slid out of her into my hands.

I grasped at the slippery child. Covered in slime that looked like blood and spit, it coughed and sputtered into a horrible cry, a wail, as if Eve's bellows had been put into it.

Eve propped herself up. "Let me see. Give me the child."

I lifted the screaming creature from the sleeping mat and handed it to her.

"Bring me a soft cloth and warm water."

She pulled the new little one to herself. I held the dangling vine that went from the child and back into her. As I did, I realized the child was male. Whether the child would be one or the other had not occurred to me.

I didn't remember talking with her about it. I thought it would be a mix, part her and part me. But why would it be any different than the other creatures. I asked her about it later. "I never doubted it would be a woman child." We were both surprised.

As I returned with the water and once again held the vine, a final part came from within her. I recalled seeing this with the sheep as well. They took these parts and moved them away from their lambs with their teeth. I guessed here too, this part was not needed.

I held it up, scooped between my hands like the innards of a melon. "All this is attached to the child," I said as she stroked the child, cleaning him.

"Cut it off," she said.

I pointed to the fleshy vine near where it was attached to the mass. "Cut? ... Where? Here?"

She pointed back up, just next to the pucker in the child's middle, from where the vine grew. "No, here. Leave just a little."

"The new one doesn't need it?"

She didn't answer. She had stopped cleaning the child and was looking down at him. In a whisper of joy she said, "Look! He is sucking my breast!"

As our baby man suckled for the first time, without asking her further, with no skill or confidence, I trimmed the vine with a sharp flint, leaving only a stub at the dimple in his middle, sticking out from him.

This all made growing rye seem simple.

She slept the entire next day with the child beside her. It was the following evening that she sat with him near the cooking fire and I sat with them too, holding his hand. I looked into the face of this child, this one born outside Eden. Would his birth have been easier under the tree, like mine? Would an angel have attended her, one prepared for the task? Would the birds have lined the boughs in the morning light and sung at his coming? I bent forward and looked in his eyes; instead of the light of Eden I saw the glow of the fire.

As we had waited so long, I had saved several furs for the child, so he was wrapped in these as his tiny fingers cupped the tip of my thumb.

"What will we call him?" I asked her.

"He is a male child. He needs a name that sounds like a man," she said.

"How about Mane? It sounds like man but speaks of the wild, a lion even."

"I don't know. I don't think I want to name my child after a part of a beast."

"Then what sounds do you like?" I asked.

"I like the sound the tongue makes ... the clicking sound."

"You mean like carve or cane?"

"Yes ... like cane. Cane. That is lovely."

I did like it very much, the sound of it.

Since we had come to the sea I had been forming again the marking of our words. From my memory of the angel and the days of naming the animals, and like the outlines of her belly in the sand, I had begun to write the sounds that we made when we spoke.

I needed to determine how to form his name. "C-a-n-e, is that how we will do it?"

"C-a-n-e," she repeated. "Can you make it different in some way?"

"What do you mean?"

"Somehow different. Use new symbols to form the word. Something just for him."

"K-a-n-e?" I asked.

"I think instead put an i in it. C-a-i-n."

"Cain, I have it. That is it."

"Cain, baby Cain," she whispered over him. And in this she named him, she made him her own.

No mother or father has used the name since.

Her attention was wholly devoted to Cain. I sat with the two of them for the first week, but I was less my firstborn's doting father and more her aid. Cain emptied himself into his furs many times a day. I took the furs out to the shore and rinsed them in the surf, hanging them in the sun to dry. I brought in the dry ones so that she could swaddle him again. I loved this beautiful baby, but from across the room. I was not like a father, holding him and speaking to him. I was a servant.

Where I had a place of my own was in my work, so as he got older this is where I went most days. I spent time mending the house of wear from wind and sun, sometimes on the roof weaving into it new sheaves of grass, other times tending to the sand and earthen mounds built up around its walls. I worked most days from sun to moon, tending as well the fields and the orchard that was in its third season. The sea became a new wilderness as I fished the deeper inlets along our coast. In time I learned of the tides and the creatures in them. I made my first net of hemp and learned to toss it, using the wind to open it over the water. I brought home what I pulled from its depths.

Eve was very good at taking these raw goods and turning them into evening delights. She minced the fish, balled it up, brushed it with pepper and oil and wrapped each ball in seaweed. She boiled these in sea water over the fire. But after we ate she turned back to Cain. I drank wine from my grapes and went in to sleep alone.

She came to bed, often in the hours just before dawn and always with the boy in her arms.

"I have gotten a child. The Maker has seen to it."

I woke to her speaking to herself, to the child. Refusing to move, to fully wake, I lay still and opened my eyes to look at her. In the gray-blue shadows of dawn she sat in the lounge I had made for her at the foot of the bed, a large basket lined with grasses and topped with animal skins. She had lit a wick using an ember from last evening's fire and had lifted the baby from his box. He had not made a sound, none I heard anyway. His mouth made a perfect oval suction around her nipple, his chin bobbing as he sucked. He established a rhythm and then stopped, still, as if asleep, and then started again with quick pulls as if to catch up on those trickles he had missed.

"You don't own the boy," I said. "He belongs to The Maker. We are only entrusted with him."

She was startled. I don't think she knew I was awake. But she had heard me and I was glad. She was treating this child as if she had invented him, made him herself.

I had said what I was thinking, but it sounded prepared. Everything I said that spoke of the days in the birthland, the days with The Maker, sounded as if I was quoting from an ancient story, the language stilted and rote.

I got up, stood at the edge of the bed and stepped over to a hollow gourd, dipping my hands in and bringing water to my face. The tips of my fingers prodded the puffy sacks of skin under my eyes.

"Well," she said, "I have certainly done my part."

Her part indeed, I thought.

In these long hours alone my anger flowed quiet and slow like a hot underground stream; my anger at her for her part, her part in losing Eden. And now I was again pushed to the side. Again she had taken her place and I was left standing behind her. Her role as my helper and mate had faded like the color of a dying fish.

"You have done your part," I said without turning to her.

"I hold hope in my arms while regret slips through your fingers."

She lowered her chin and kissed Cain's bald head. Lingering, her lips pressed against his scalp, she pulled him close. "You'll crush that ugly snake's head, won't you?" His suckle relaxed as his nose flattened against her breast. She placed all her trust in this tiny offspring, this helpless, soft, eater. Her power was in giving life to this one.

But I had not seen her so content since our first seasons together. And I envied her that.

Following his birth I had marked his days, one by one, with small charcoal hashes on the outside of the house by the door. Cain was nearly seventy days old and still could not walk.

We had seen other young creatures respond to the need to walk and we thought Cain should do the same. When we were born we knew how to walk. We worked endlessly with him, holding him upright, attempting to introduce him to his legs. He would only lie on his back and grab at his toes, pulling his feet down, even into his mouth!

"Maybe this is a good sign?" I asked, pointing to Cain lying back in the grass, his tongue on his toe. "He has met his feet."

"I'm afraid to think so," she said.

I came in from the sea in the evenings and rubbed his hips and knees, massaging into him a mixture of herbs and ginger that Eve had boiled while he napped earlier in the day. We did this hoping to bring strength to his fatty, short legs. I alternately massaged and held him up, moving his legs in a walking motion. As I worked on him, Eve sat beside me and cried.

"Why is our child lame?" she asked.

I worked at his hips as he dozed and cooed, night after night.

One afternoon he rolled over and within a few moons he had propped himself up on his hands and knees. We were certain that he was going to gather himself up and put his feet against the ground. Instead, he shuffled on his palms and knees, chasing us from one room to the next like a turtle.

It seemed he was not only lame but stupid. He grasped at hot coals, forcing us to pull him up just before he reached them. He scooted up to the smallest trees, not bigger around than his own thumb, and pulled himself up on them, leaning on them as if they could support him. He toppled over onto his back, his legs and arms quaking in the air as he screamed.

The same mouth which nursed at Eve's breast now became a holder for everything he could fit and guide into it. Concern over our little cripple was no longer that he was lame but that he might burn or choke himself while we weren't watching. We began to sit with him. One of us stood guard over him at all times, even as he slept. The boy had come to us broken. "It is because we opened the fruit under the tree," I said.

One winter morning while Eve was still sleeping, I was bent down at the cooking fire, stoking the embers from the night before. I was exhausted because I had sat by his sleeping mat all night. As I jabbed at the ashes and blew a few tired puffs across them, I felt a pounce on my backside. I held still and swung my head around, my neck extended, my eyes rolled to their corners. To my delight there stood Cain, his knees locked and wobbling, his back swaying in and out and his fists clenching my cloak.

"Eve!" I called, while also trying to hold my voice so as not to startle him.

"Yes?" Her faint reply from our room.

"Come here!"

She walked into the room. As if on demand Cain looked up at her, let go of me and turned. He took five steps before sinking into her outstretched arms.

The fire flared as we sat on the floor around it. Eve cried as she hugged and kissed our newly walking little boy. I wept too. At last our son could walk! Now perhaps we could give our attention to why he had not yet spoken to us in our language, why his nearly toothless mouth only made half sounds and gurgles. Cain squirmed to get out of Eve's grasp, our excitement and tears invisible to him.

That evening, for summoning such strength and overcoming his weakness, I blessed him. We celebrated his victory with praise offerings on the altar. We burned grains and sprinkled wine, something we had not done since our first tiny harvest outside the birth-land. Eve fed Cain the way she had since the first anniversary of his birth, she chewed his food for him and then taking it from her mouth she tucked it in his cheek for him to swallow.

It was not until our second son Abel came to us that we understood this late walking and talking was like the normal maturing of wine. Still my blessing remained on Cain. I am able to look back now with an old and steady love for him, my first son.

As Cain grew, he stepped out with me for short periods, usually to assist with planting or pruning, his little hands rummaging in the dirt at the base of a vine. The way he created a mound around the stem of a grape seedling, cupping his palms to pat it down made my way of planting seem brutal and unloving. But our time together never lasted. Eve fetched him to be with her. "Cain, Cain my little helper, mother calls you."

He heard her and jumped up. "Here I am, here I am!" as he ran to her. She lifted and carried him as they walked away toward the house to peel vegetables or weave. The boy was hers.

But at the birth of Abel, two harvests later, I was afforded a companion. As I worked the stone fences or moved our herds from one pasture to another, Abel waddled along behind me. Before he could do even that, I made a little seat out of bark and I strapped him atop a goat and took him with me. We spent all day, every day together. He could guide sheep and separate goats the day he learned to walk. I made him a long, thin staff from a palm and he used this to guide the animals, most of which were as tall as he was. In time I taught him to sheer sheep, to birth them, and how to read the land and sky to see the first signs of a change in the season. There was nothing I knew that I didn't try to pass on to him.

Except the past.

I couldn't discuss that. Not yet. The events of Eden were too large for conversation. I wasn't ready to talk about it and I certainly wasn't ready for the questions that might come of hearing such things.

And for a long time I was able to avoid it.

Until an evening meal, when the boys were in their sixth and eighth years.

Cain started the conversation. He looked at Eve and then at me, keeping his eyes finally on me. "Do you have a mother and father? Where are they?" He asked as if he knew something, had an idea there was more to our story than to his.

Abel looked up, listening. I let the question sit between us for too long as I tried to build an answer that would not simply lead Cain to more questions.

Eve was quicker to answer. "We didn't have a mother, we only have a father and He lives far away. He made us with His hands."

Cain looked confused. "He made you?"

"And all that you see. He is called The Maker," said Eve.

Abel spoke. "Does He ever play with you?"

"He did when we were young, but now He lets us play with you instead." I hoped that what I was saying, what we were saying, would satisfy their young minds.

"Will we ever see Him?" asked Cain.

"He said He would see us again," said Eve, "but it has been more moons than you and I can count. We don't know when that will be. But when He does come you will get to see Him."

Both boys had more questions. We hadn't told them about Eden or why we weren't still living there. I assumed we'd wait until they were a bit older and let the questions they would someday ask draw it out of us.

I had no idea such a conversation would never happen.

The next morning I got up and found Eve weaving a lunch basket for each of the boys. She paused and looked up.

"I am glad you found a way to answer them last night," I said. "I didn't know what to say."

She went back to her weaving. "They're satisfied now, but they'll have more questions."

"I know. I have thought of this and I dread it." But this was not what I wanted to talk to her about. I sat down next to her. "I want to tell you ... I need more time with Cain. There are things I must teach them both."

"What am I to do? Be alone all day here in this house with only the fire and some weaving grass?"

"No, you can come with us. We will take fish from the sea and milk the goats." I didn't think she was going to join us in any such thing. But I was offering.

"What will I do with all those smelly beasts?"

But I kept at it to win my point. "Come with us to the sea, then. You can enjoy the air as we work."

"I don't care for the sea as much as you do, Adam. These herbs and flowers, the gardens and paths, these are my places. Cain cares deeply for the plants too. You've seen him."

"Abel has learned so much already. Just give me a few hours at the end of each day with Cain as well so that he, too, can learn."

She shrugged and started weaving again. "Fine. Go ahead and take Cain along. But if he shows no interest, don't force. He is only a child."

There were three skills that both children needed, and so I focused on these: herding, fishing, and planting.

The herding was the most fun for them. I gave Cain a thin staff like I'd made for Abel. I then put a small flock of lambs out in the pen to graze in the short grass.

I pulled the boys to either side of me. "Your job is to hold your staff out and gather the lambs. Gather them like pebbles on a flat rock."

They both looked up at me. "You mean gather them to each other," said Abel. He had clarified my instruction to show that he knew this one.

"Right, gather them together," I said.

Cain looked down at the staff in his hand and up at me.

Abel continued. "Cain, you go that way and I'll go this way."

"Can I strike them?" asked Cain, holding his staff up high. He started to bring the staff down toward the head of one of the lambs.

I jumped and grabbed the boy's arm stopping him. "No!" I yelled, and jerked the staff from his hand. Cain looked up at me. In his eyes I saw not embarrassment or fear, just a stare.

Abel started laughing. "Just nudge them at the side and they'll move away from the stick. You can push them along that way."

Cain did not laugh. He looked at the stick. I handed it back to him slowly and he squeezed it tight with his fist. He pushed down on the stick so that it bent against the ground. "You start," he said to Abel without looking at him.

So they began, Cain to one side and Abel to the other. At first the lambs didn't notice the boys, but soon enough they did. One started bleating and set the whole flock off. The boys both started to laugh as the lambs jumped along at the tip of their staffs. Soon the lambs were piled up on top of each other and the boys were running around the squirming mound of wool, staffs over their heads laughing and jumping. It is an image I'll carry with me for the rest of my life.

Fishing was next. I had made a net out of vine for them, like mine, but smaller. I showed it to the boys while we were still at the house. "This is a net. This is what we use to catch the fish of the sea. We throw it and it sinks down on top of them."

Playfully I threw the net up into the breeze. It spun and lifted and came down over the boys' heads. Abel panicked and started to cry, clawing at the net. Cain started swinging around wildly trying to break free, slamming into Abel in the process.

"I'm sorry. Here my little men." I said as I pulled it off of them. I had thought they'd enjoy it. I decided to distract them by heading down to the shore. "Let's go catch some fish!"

Abel sniffled and Cain looked out at the sea.

They followed me down the path and onto the shore. We climbed up onto the rocks that lined the run of the beach. As they stood and watched I threw the net out into the water and it disappeared.

"Where did it go?" asked Cain.

"Here." I showed them the rope in my hand. "This is tied to the net."

"Oh." They both realized at the same time how the net worked as I then began to pull it toward us.

The surface jumped and thrashed as I pulled the net into shallower water. Both boys grabbed the rope and began to pull our catch to shore. The net slipped up onto the rock and I began to lift it away. Cain and Abel gathered at my sides staring. We had five fish, one was twice the size of the others, several crabs, a strand of hearty seaweed, and a small octopus.

I lifted the seaweed away. "We'll salt and dry this. It is very good to eat."

"What is that?" said Cain pointing at the octopus. They had both seen and eaten fish and crab, but this was new.

I picked up the octopus as its parts wrapped around my wrist and the back of my hand.

"Can we touch him?" asked Abel.

"Sure. Just be careful that you don't poke his eyes."

Each of them took a leg in their hand and felt the shape of the soft creature as it inched across their skin.

"Can we keep him?" asked Abel. Cain was standing back looking at the fish.

"No, little man, I don't think so. He needs to be here in the sea. But he is still yours, even in here."

Abel lifted the small creature from my hand and held him as he walked toward the edge of the rock. Kneeling, he put his arm down in the water. The octopus gently slid off of Abel's hand and pushed against his palm as it dove away. Abel knelt there on the rock. "I liked him. I hope we see him again."

I gathered the fish and crabs into my fish basket, laid the net out on the rocks in the sun to dry, and walked with the boys toward home.

As we came up to the house I showed Cain some pepper plants I was growing. Abel was poking at the fish in the basket. He was most interested in their eyes.

"What do you notice about these plants?" I asked Cain.

"They are small."

"That's true. What else."

"They are lined up in a row."

"I planted them in a row. Do you know why?"

"So you could find them?"

"Yes, I didn't want to lose them in the other plants. But there is another reason."

"What is it?"

"See, in this way I can easily walk between the rows and I have a place to put my harvesting basket."

Cain looked back and forth at the row of plants.

"My Father taught me to do that," I said.

"Can I tell mother about this idea?"

"Sure, young man, sure you can."

He took off running into the house.

Later that evening, after dinner, I gathered the boys while Eve was getting ready for bed.

"One more thing for today, boys. This is called wine. It is made from the grapes. It is a gift from The Maker. Would you like to try a little bit?" I poured a splash into each of their cups.

Abel picked it up and smelled it while Cain stared down at his cup. Then, at the exact same time they picked up their cups and sipped. Their little mouths puckered.

"Can we put some molasses in it?" asked Cain.

Abel set down his cup. "Yes, maybe some molasseses? It is really sour." Abel was still struggling with long words like molasses.

I sat back and laughed. They were a wonderful pair of boys who were quickly becoming young men.

Over the next several seasons I taught them to perfect filleting a fish. They practiced on small ones until both of them could dress any fish we caught. As they grew, Abel remained attentive, suggesting new ways we could buckle down our sheep for shearing or set hollowed-out logs end to end to move the water. We protected our herds from hyena, or worse, the great birds. Abel began to build latticed roofs over the pens of our animals to protect them from the swooping hunters.

Cain was more interested in plants and would take ones he found and leave us to return home to Eve. Together he and she planted them, in rows, in one of their gardens.

It was during these times that Abel and I hunted smaller game for a bit of red meat with our fish. Many times Abel would ask Cain to join us. Cain would always say how he found Abel's love of the hunt irksome.

One evening Abel stepped to the edge of the field as Cain worked. Abel bent to touch a melon, trying to make sense of what kept Cain working in the dirt all day. Cain looked up and saw Abel. "Keep your blood-stained fingers off them," he snapped.

I was clearing brush from along the back of the vineyard. I had heard the exchange and watched as Abel turned away and was now skipping rocks, pitching them across a pond at the edge of the woods. I also heard Eve talking to Cain. She had joined him working at the edge of the field. It was his twelfth year. He was nearly a man.

"There is power in the sun," she said.

"Power," said Cain.

She knelt beside him among the plants. "Yes. It shows favor on these upturned leaves and our worshiping, upturned faces."

He looked at her deeply, following her words with his eyes, and then turned toward the sun. Lifting his hand to block it out and saying nothing, he closed his eyes. She remained beside him as they basked in the sunlight.

This was not the first time I had heard such silliness, and I did not like it. The sun was not special, it was not caring. Its light did not carry love. It was the largest light in the sky, created for us and before us. It was not interested in our affections.

Late that night as I came to bed, I woke Eve to talk to her. The boys slept.

"You have been in the wine." Her first words to me. I had not said anything.

"I have had a little. Why do you always make a matter of it? A bit of wine is nothing."

"Yes it is. You are always in the drink. You get a cut and out it runs before your blood."

"I was created perfect, without a fault. But I've become something else. And so have you. You were there when it happened." I didn't leave her time to respond. "This is a waste of time. We need to talk about Cain."

The soft scent of oils hung in the air. She had taken her bath and had just fallen asleep when I came in. She sat up in the bed, naked, her knees folded under her. Perhaps she had been waiting for me.

"You smell of rotten grapes and dirty hair," she said. "Why did you wake me?"

"What are you trying to do to Cain?"

"I'm teaching him the beauty of the ground and sky."

"No, you're telling him lies. 'The sun favors our upturned faces?' Lighting candles to seduce the mists? What is this silliness?"

"You are a drunkard. You imagine things. I am pretending, I am playing with a child! What do you think? That I am some lost soul you must come in here in your stupor to save?"

I leaned in. "Cain is not a child. He's almost a man. He needs to be taught, not filled with fanciful stories. I am teaching him what he needs to know in order to rule over the land. He is my heir."

"You already keep Abel as your sheep dog, his gentleness squandered in your rule over the land. Rule. What do you rule? You rule only over grapes."

The back of my hand caught her cheek. The crack of flesh hitting flesh split the air. She fell back on the bed.

"You tell Cain lies! These are things you've made up!" I told her. "The Maker made me to rule and He made you to help me rule. You are taking over with Cain. You need to find your place back at my side."

"Where do you get these ideas? They come with the wine." She did not cry or cringe as she spoke. "I've heard all this before. I hear it every time you are in the wine. You talk of who you were made to be. How you were made to rule. Without the wine you vanish, like some mistreated runt, into the fields and down the shoreline." Then soft, such that I had to strain to hear her, "You rule over nothing. Not even over a naked woman in her bed."

Oren of Susa: Giving Life

Adam is exhausted and emotionally worn thin. As he told me of him and Eve he slid to the edge of his bed and sat up. Now he lies back again as if a great task is behind him. I set down my lap desk and stretch out my legs in front of me. The fire which was started earlier in the afternoon by a servant is dying down. I begin to think of something warm to drink when Adam asks, "You've told me you have no wife, but do you have children?"

"Yes, I do. A son."

"So tell me."

I sit back and cross my legs, giving in to the story. "Soon after Liana, there was another woman, Kivah. She lived in Susa and was a few years older than me. We knew of each other's families—Susa was only a village in those days—and had met a few times growing up.

"I was so deeply sad from losing Liana. She knew what had happened. Everyone in Susa knew. Kivah had known Liana quite well when they were little girls. Kivah was

241

wonderful in comforting me. We spent evenings together, walking, talking. She had no husband but she spoke of children, and pointed out babies anytime there was one near. For more than a year she gave me comfort. After several months together she told me she was pregnant. I was overwhelmed at the sudden thought of becoming a father. In ignorance I had not considered that this could happen. But I knew she wanted a child and this new life was an apt response to the loss I'd had."

"So you had a son," says Adam.

"She did. Kivah left before the child was born, left Susa with her newly widowed mother and moved to a city on the other side of the twin rivers to be near her mother's family. I was devastated. I missed her. I missed the comfort she brought to me, our friendship. I had come to love her. But her leaving was for the best. I was young. My parents, my family had no idea of the affair or the child. They never knew. I would have had no idea what to do with a son. I am sure she knew this.

"I knew nothing of her or the child for thirty-five years. For a couple of years after she left I wondered about her and the child. But soon it seemed like another lifetime, those years with Liana and then Kivah. I was busy with the tablet house and the students. My father was quickly becoming an old man and was leaving the running of the house to me.

"Then one morning, just the spring before last, I received a sealed letter by carrier.

"The moments she and I had shared came rushing back at me. Kivah explained she was well, although older— 'aren't we all?' she wrote—and that the child, my son, was in fact a market dealer and did business in Susa, should I want to seek him out.

"I walked once a week around the market and tried to spot him. I looked for myself as a younger man and then I looked for her features—as I remembered them—in the faces of the dealers. I tried to spot him. Finally, I wrote back to her. I did not promise to seek him out, I only asked his name. When her letter came with his name, Teel, I could not resist. I went the next day to the market. I only had to ask once before I was pointed to him."

Adam looks at me. He has been listening to every word. "How did your son respond to you when you found him and when you spoke after so long?"

"I stepped into the shade of his market tent and asked to speak with him. 'Of course,' he said. We sat together at the back of his tent as if an agreement on trade was pending. She had written of his success in moving goods and his expertise in matters of the marketplace. He had become well known among the merchants.

"I decided not to explain it. I simply showed him the letters from his mother. I watched as he read them. I sat across from him until he looked up at me. He gave me that first knowing look, reading and realizing I was his father. For the first time my son looked at me. We were two men, strangers who knew nothing of each other, who now shared this one secret from deep in our pasts. He said she had told him about me when he was a little boy and again more recently, 'She told me you were the scribe there in Susa.' He had considered seeking me out, as I would be easy enough to find, but was unsure. 'Will this scribe want to see me?' he had asked himself.

"With these opening words it was plain to me that he had Kivah's kindness, her warmth and openness. This man who sat across from me was made more of her than of me, and for this I was both grateful and moved in affection toward him. This first meeting was brief, as we both struggled to find a place to start. But we agreed to meet each month and within the year we soon found a familiarity existed between us, one that neither of us could describe. And I became a father for the first time—my heart chiseled open by my only son.

"It was from Teel I learned at one of our meetings that Kivah was gone. That she had not woken one morning. I told him maybe I should have gone with him to see her. He said not to let that regret take hold, for it had been she who left me. Like her, he knew what to say to my grief. And so in this again he and I found another place where our selves were stitched together. Our relationship grew deeper. We were the survivors of our family."

"Do you see also yourself in Teel?"

"I do, yes, but more Kivah. I see her in his face, especially when he is hard at work and focused on his business. She, too, was diligent in even the simplest task."

I can see the memory of Eve wash over Adam's face and leave again. I've learned to see his features soften and turn inward when she is on his mind.

And as I see it this time I wonder. How can I ease this man's mind? Does The Maker intend me to do more? Is there some other thing? Perhaps The Maker has some action I can take to offer him comfort? The idea comes like a shaft of light. Surely there is more for me here than to finish making the letters of his lifetime.

I continue. "The great reward was at our last meeting before I came here. Teel brought my grandson to meet me—a lovely boy of seven years. My grandson sat on my knee. I could not have imagined such a thing. This boy is as smart as most men three times his age."

Adam sits quietly, still looking at me, but he is no longer looking at me. He has forgotten I'm in the room.

Chapter Twelve

Hoisted Him Up and Stretched Him Out

We reclined around the dinner fire. Talk slowed. Cain had been restless all evening. I assumed it was due to another spat with Abel. As I thought about this and how I might tell them, for the hundredth time in a hundred moons, that they must learn to care for one another and they were each other's keeper and must find it in themselves to listen first and speak second, Cain told us he had heard the voice of The Maker.

Our heads all rose like bubbles to the surface of a pool. I stopped chewing and pushed the chunk of lamb into my cheek.

"Are you sure?" I asked. "Were any of us with you?"

"No. I was alone, cutting back some of the arbor near the east path."

I kept going. "Was The Maker present with you ... could you see Him?"

Eve had stopped eating too. She had put down her bowl, scooting it away from her, her eyes on Cain. Dinner was no longer of interest.

"No," said Cain, "There was no one there, just the words, the sound of them."

We sat in silence. I thought of when The Maker had been seeking us, how the wind had stirred all around us, carrying His voice into my ear while I lay against the earth, the tang of the nectar in my mouth.

Abel slid forward and was staring as if Cain might take on the voice's figure right before us.

"What did the voice say?" I asked.

"Things I have only thought. Things I have told no one."

"Go on then," said Abel, his face flashing with pious excitement, "what did The Maker of All say to you?"

"Shut your mouth!" Cain demanded, snapping a quick glance at him.

"Abel, sit back," I said. But I had to know too. "My son, my first-born, tell me. Repeat for us the words of the Voice."

Cain stared at the fire between us. "The Voice said, 'Why do you approach Me with such groaning? Do you think I will not accept your best fruits if given to Me with open hands? Come to Me with your best, not only your best fruit. If not, the path of darkness desires you.'"

I looked at Eve. She did not look at me, but instead asked the question we were all thinking.

"How do you know this was The Maker? How do you know these were not your own thoughts, of your own mind's making?"

"Because it fell on me like moonlight in a clearing. The Voice came in all around me and I could not turn away from it."

Abel put his hand on Cain's shoulder but Cain yanked out from under his brother's touch, as if from a hunter's trap. He stood, poured himself another tumbler of wine, drank it fast, and refilled again. He turned and stood over Abel. "You are not my judge, nor is my experience some wonder from The Maker for you to delight in." He left, leaving us sitting and looking after him.

Eve started to get up. I touched her arm and stood. "Let him go," I said, "he needs to be alone. He will come back."

Abel turned and watched Cain wander off into the dusk shadows. "I will try to speak to him in the morning."

The following midday I came into an empty house. I assumed she was out walking, as she often was, wandering between the orchards, looking for wild berries and quail eggs. I came in having spent the early hours making preparations to build a wall along the edge of the sea. I had collected stones and stacked them in piles by size and shape. The day had started out warm. It was now hot and required pacing oneself.

Abel had spent the earliest part of the day working with me. He, too, was collecting stones for a small house he was constructing not far from ours. I saw some of the timbers he used for the base of the house. With troughs dug, and their mass half buried in a mix of sand, lime, and clay, they were a sound frame in which to set the stone floor. It was not to be a large dwelling, but it was stouter than my hands had ever wrought.

Abel had shown himself to be devout, much more so than any of us. On the same site as this building he had set up an altar where he went daily to sacrifice a beast of one sort or another, giving in worship that which to him was pure. I had told him of sacrifice in the birthland. I had told them both within the last season, but Abel had taken the past as a sort of seed. In him had sprouted a belief, a worship of The Maker. In this he succeeded where I had failed. He gladly took the mantel of believer, on all our behalves. He had found the peace we felt at that first sacrifice in Eden. Where I had become self-reliant, and had turned to the land and what it might offer me, he led us toward the way of The Maker.

Cain at first joined Abel for these sacrifices, although neither Eve nor I were sure why. It was as if he felt he must follow along so as not to be outdone by his younger brother.

He responded as if the task was being set upon his shoulders, and he must force himself to bear up under it. But the meaning seemed to be lost for him. He would bring baskets of fruit or grain, or a pot of oil or wine to sacrifice. He did not see Abel's animal sacrifice as a version of this same gift. Abel's sacrifices disgusted Cain. He thought they were revolting. This was no secret.

I prepared my mid-day meal, thinking these thoughts, considering these boys and the last evening's conversation. After I ate I'd go out and see Cain. I was worried about him. I knew what it was like to be sought by The Maker. I wanted to let him know that.

It was just as I took my first bite that her screams met my ears. Horrible angry screams, screams like I've never heard since, came from somewhere outside the house. I jumped back to my feet, tipping my bowl onto the floor. I called for the boys but knew at once that they were not in the house either.

Over and over Eve's cry pierced the hot air. I ran outside and around the house, stopping, holding my breath to listen. There it came again, louder, more urgent, from across the pasture. I spun and ran, my feet leading, twisting my body. My heels sank into soft, pillowed moss and grass-covered clumps of soil. Churning across the field a small rise in the pasture kept her out of view at first, but the next moment there she was, across the pasture and into the nearside field, a vision sliding toward me. On her hands and knees, she screamed, her head up and pulled back.

The meal baskets she had brought out for the boys now held nothing, their handles tipped into the dirt, contents strewn on either side of me, never to be eaten, marking my path. I ran faster, stumbling at the last, but staying on my feet through awkward flailing strides. The image of Abel lying in the dirt and her struggling to pick him up, jostled about in my vision, washed out in the bright midday sunlight.

As I came to her she struggled to her feet and began to run further yet, as if my coming released her to go. It was then I saw Cain, beyond her, running further still.

I fell to my knees and gathered Abel just as she had, cradling his head. Thick, dark blood pasted my hand and forearm, spread by his beautiful curls now matted with dirt. His shoulders sagged as I lifted him. I started to speak. For a moment his eyes seemed to focus on mine. I said words, comforting words in a tone of panic. I looked up at Eve still running and back again, back into his face just as his eyes rolled up toward the blue sky, empty. His lips went slack, parted and pale, no breath passed between them, only a deep, wet, gurgle.

I stared at him and all else fell to the sides of my vision. I kept watching him, my face just a thumb's width from his. All action was drained from his features. Then I saw it, the color. The color fading from his cheeks and from his forehead, the color melting and pulling away like a receding tide. And I knew. I screamed now, sobbing and pulling him close to me, struggling to lift and hold him, his body in all its weight, heavy in my arms.

I pulled him up, my back arched as he slipped in my arms. My boy. My boy. His life drifted off toward the clouds like vapor. My boy.

Looking up again, I saw that Eve had stopped chasing Cain. She stood hunched over, trying to catch her breath. Cain passed the edge of the field and into the trees, his garden pick in hand, running away from us. And then he was gone.

She turned, looked at me, then collapsed, wailing and beating the sod in rage.

Tears blurred my vision as I dug the grave. The dirt appeared before me in waves of mud.

We had picked a spot just to the back of a small stand of trees and had carried his body off the field, down the hillside, past the stable gate and into the shade. I had laid out several tree limbs between a pair of stumps while Eve gathered water, tallow, wood ash, and a cloth. She now washed Abel's naked body as it lay upon this crude table. I had hoisted him up and stretched him out. I had placed a loaf-shaped rock under his neck to steady his broken head.

We had talked about it.

"He is gone. He will not come back to this body," I said. "We must place it somewhere."

She looked at me as if it was a surprise. "Place it? You mean put it away?"

I remembered how when my dog had a treasured item he hid it, burying it in the earth, in a location known only to him.

"Yes, we must."

"Let no wild animal find him ..." She paused, looking up at me, pleading. One of her wet, soapy hands hung suspended, dripping onto her feet, the other lay limp across Abel's lifeless and ashen knee.

"We will bury him, put him in the earth," I said.

"But there are no caves here."

"I will make a cave in the earth, a hold in which his body can lie and mingle with the dust."

"I want to wash and wrap him." More tears came, her brown eyes drowning in them. "I love ... loved him."

"Yes," I said, "I know. You can wash and wrap him."

This woman who had been presented to me by The Maker Himself, so young and perfect, now looked so tired, so worn.

Even old.

I thought about her and Cain. He was so much hers. She had laid claim to him as soon as he was born. He was part of her soul. And then I thought of how she had told me only a few days earlier that she was pregnant. There was another person in this scene yet hidden away. Without words I dug, my stone splitting the dirt. And she washed, creating mounds of tiny bubbles with each pass of the wet linen.

Out of the corner of my eye I caught a glimpse of Abel's feet hanging over the edge of the boards. I thought of the temple foundation, of the stack of stones I would find the next morning on the shore—carefully sorted, all the same size. I would leave them. Leave them stacked just as he had left them.

I kept dreaming, wishing he'd wake. He'd pop up, a huge smile on his face, the soap running down his chest, asking us what we were doing. It would be like him to ask such a question. Eve would scream again, for joy, and hug him, fall on him, nearly tipping him off the boards. Then, as he swung his legs and stepped onto the grass I would hand him his cloak as we laughed and retold our error. Cain would return just then with a basket of herbs and onions.

And after dinner I would return to this spot and fill in this silly, mistaken hole.

Oren of Susa: Tell Him This

Reclining under his portico and looking out at the sea, I watch Adam as he smokes from a wooden bowl. There is a tree leaf in it that eases the pain in his gut—"The pain feels like fingers clawing at me from the inside."

All I've written thus far lies on the table between us. Adam is beginning to look through it like he said he wanted to when we first started, but he doesn't read it for more than a few minutes at a time. At first I think it is the sickness that slows his reading, but as I watch him I think he's too shaken by the telling—or by seeing it laid out before him in writing. It is all fresh again.

"You are thinking of Cain?" I ask.

He nods. "Yes, but my experience was not like yours, Oren. Having children, after all that had happened, was a reminder of loss."

"I know many fathers who enjoy their children, who care for them and love them. It is not pain for them."

Adam leans forward, his elbows on his knees. "Of course, so do I. But as for me I knew too much. Being a father was so little joy. And there is no reason to think it could be any joy now, after so long."

For all Adam is, I see at this moment sitting before me only an old man, like any other, who is far removed from a son he still loves. "You don't know," I say. "If The Maker wills it."

"I have never thought ... of a grandson. I've never thought of Cain having a son." I see Adam's eyes well up and he is gone for several minutes, looking into the fire.

I think of my son and my grandson and I am warmed with thankfulness—for the first time I am overcome with pure gratitude to The Maker that I have been given Teel. I want such a thing for Adam.

"The stories you told me of your times with the boys, they were lovely. You seem to have enjoyed your first two sons."

"I did enjoy them, but for so long my joy has been dampened by the thick oil of grief."

"Do you regret having had Cain and Abel?"

"No. That is not it. It is something else, something more." Adam lifts himself up in his chair. "I regret every death, Oren, every misery, every word ever spoken in anger by any man or woman who has ever lived. And it is not a regret wondering what I could have done differently. It is a regret that remembers the exact moment when I let evil seep into this world. And it is regret, too, for me, that I turned all I had into this, that I altered my life from one of hourly delights to a timeless and steady sorrow."

"I wonder, Adam, if you overstate it a little." I am

trying to help him past all this, or at least further along through it.

He lays his head back. "I don't," he says.

There comes a knock on the post at the corner of the room. We are interrupted by household staff with questions about this detail and that—how many cattle should be butchered for the winter months? "Two. One large and one small." Would he like his regular tour of the pastures? He takes the tour each new moon. "No. Let's forgo the tour this time." Will he give the day of the chief servant's wedding to the staff as a holiday? "Yes, and the day after as well."

He turns to me. "Why not be generous, yes Oren?"

"Indeed," I say. "Why not?"

The last of the staff leave and we are alone again.

"Do you still love Cain?"

Adam pauses, following my lead back to the story.

"After we buried Abel I slept on the ground in that field and waited for Cain. I stayed there day after day until the new moon. He is my child. You know, Oren, what a son means to a father, no matter the past."

"I do, Adam." And I do. I know how empty I was without my son—or how much poorer I was before I met him.

"Two winters ago," says Adam, "I was told by a trader that Cain is still alive, that he is living in a city on the other side of the sea. They say he is avoided by many for his past. They all know who he is and no one wants to get close to him. No one does him harm, yet finding good things, like the love of a woman and work, is difficult."

"You are concerned about him."

"I am worried for him, yes. I know what it is like to be a man with a past.

"Cain was my firstborn son. I have memories of him as a baby, as a child, on my knee playing with my beard as we sat among the olive trees or running with him in the tall grass as he chased young goats. My love for him is set in those things, in those times."

The idea comes to me—I can do for Adam what he cannot do for himself because of who he is and the old man he has become. I will not attract the attention and notice he no doubt would. "Do you want to speak with him, to reach out to Cain and perhaps even see him again? I could help you with that."

Adam looks at me as if I've provided an answer to a long-sought riddle.

"Perhaps I could go," I say, "and try to see him, talk to him. Maybe he thinks of you."

Adam puts the pipe on the table between us. He struggles to his feet. It is the first time I've seen him stand in weeks. "Might you do that?" he asks with his back turned to me.

"Would you like me to?"

Adam sits again on the edge of his bed. He pulls his legs up, bending and lifting them, and settles back against his pillow. He is out of breath. I wonder if he's stood for the last time.

There is only silence. I am sure Adam is working it out. I remember working it out for myself. He is trying to get beyond the emotions this has stirred. He's moving past all that to the first meeting. Is this a past he wants to unbutton?

"Yes."

"I will try then," I say. "I will make every effort to contact him for you."

"Your part is the easy part."

"You're right. It is. So what will you have me write?"

Adam looks at the floor between us, composing what he will say. I pick up my lap desk and settle it before me. I listen, waiting quietly for Adam.

"Tell him I never again plowed that field. Tell him I once traveled back to it and I walked out into it. Tell him it is my field, that I own what happened there. I am an ancient commander standing at the site, centuries after the din of battle has risen and floated away on the wind and been drawn up into the clouds. I walk to the spot where I held Abel's body and fell in grief over it."

Adam stops. He sinks back onto his bed. He is struggling to go on.

So I continue for him, speaking aloud as I write the words of a dying father. "There is no marker for this spot. But I know it. I know the position of the spot according to the trees to the north, those trees into which you vanished. There are unkempt flowers and grains billowing there now, plants sown by birds and wind. I imagine some of the plants are descendants of seeds your young hands spread. The field is full of life."

Adam looks up at me. He is in tears.

"Anything else you'd like me to add?" I ask.

Adam nods. "Tell him that if he will come and see me I will open my door wide to him."

I did as I said I would. Once I returned home to Susa I wrote the letter. But I held it, and I wrote also a short note. I sent this note to Cain. In it I stated that I had just spent the better part of two years with his father and I had a letter from Adam intended for him and wished to deliver it to him myself.

I was given report that my note was received by Cain and that he read it. A fistful of months passed and report came again. He would see me.

So I went. I traveled from town to town, following the direction from each scribe who had helped with the delivery of my note. I came within a half-day's walk of where Cain was reported to live and found a room with the local scribe for the night.

A student of the scribe came to me early the next morning, just before I was to travel to Cain's home.

Cain had fled to avoid meeting me.

I went anyway. I was shown to a house on the edge of the small city, at the end of a footpath in some woods. As I stood in the quiet clearing I stopped short and looked around me. I knew it was Cain's home.

I felt a lightness in my head as if I had stepped off into a vision, a revelation of what I had heard and written. The place looked as if it had been created, stone by stone, log by log from the descriptions Adam had given to me of his home in Eden. And there was a solemness, a holiness in the place that I could nearly taste and touch. This place had been set aside. It was a place of refuge.

I left the letter there. I left it under a rock at the base of a flowering vine that climbed up the front of the house.

And we wait to hear. For as of this writing there has been no response. I know only that Cain received the letter.

I tried to encourage him, the last time I saw him, but Adam wouldn't speak of it. He said nothing to me when I mentioned the waiting, and what the waiting may or may not bring. And now I don't know if he is still waiting or if I wait alone.

Chapter Thirteen

Brief Moments It Seemed Possible

After waiting nearly the same number of days as we had before, and after her belly had swelled as if the mass of it might pull her forward and cause her to topple onto it, and after her legs had swelled such that the bone of her ankles disappeared, Eve gave birth in the middle of the day, in the shade by the storehouse.

Atara came to us. I cradled her across my forearm with her feet pulled upward, her legs spread. "Look, it is a girl this time!" Eve took Atara and held her close, smoothing back her dark head of hair. As she did this I saw Eve's belly had not yet fallen. There was still a mound. I wondered for a few moments about this but I had little time to do so, for Eve had not yet started to wipe clean the new baby when the pains began again.

Eve pulled herself into a ball, nearly dropping the baby into the tall grass. I took Atara and laid her in her box, a new one I had built, and went back to Eve's side.

"What is it?"

"I don't know. The pain. It is just as it was this morning." She began panting, the sweat beaded like before on her pale forehead, cool to my touch. She cried out again and arched her back; her legs shook.

After a few moments she was able to lay back. "Look and see," she said, "see if the after-birth part has come out yet."

I got down on my knees to see. It had not. But there was ... a head! Another child was coming!

I came around to the side of her and knelt, took Eve's hand and leaned close to her.

"Eve, there is another."

She looked at me. All expression dropped out of her face.

"There is another," I said, "another child coming." I held her hand as I saw a grimace come over her from the next wave of pain.

"Another?" She began again to pant.

"Yes!"

I slipped back down to help and in moments I held the shoulders of Yaffa as she came to us.

We were four again.

Having two babies at once took all our effort. A dozen times a day I helped Eve settle back on our bed and position the babies side by side across the front of her so that they could nurse, each at a breast. At first they squirmed against each other, kicking and kneeing each other in the head and shoulders, but then they learned to roll to their sides and suckle in unison.

When they were finished they would sometimes cry and moan. We had learned with the boys that we could hold and bounce them, and so with these, too, we encouraged them to let out their air. But such loud burps for little girls! And sometimes a puddle of Eve's milk would follow. A constant flow of liquids went into them and an equally frequent mess came out.

For the first months they were confused as they slept by the sun and were awake by the moon, crying if we were not holding them. I recall the middle of one night Eve and I were each holding one of them, sitting on the floor by the cooking fire. As I sat there in my half-awake state I was startled. I heard a baby cry out from the far corner of the house. I looked over at Eve. She was staring straight ahead, eyes wide.

"Did you hear that?" I asked.

"Yes," she said.

We needed sleep.

The girls were very focused on each other. As soon as they could sit up, but before they could speak they exchanged a babbling with each other that held meaning only for them. They would sit facing each other for hours and 'talk' as they stacked small flat stones or rolled a round gourd back and forth between them.

We took the girls to the pen with us to care for the goats and sheep. They would sit at the edge of the pen as we worked. It was here that they learned to walk. They pulled themselves up on either side of one of the lambs and tottered along with it, their fists full of soft wool. The creature seemed to hardly notice their presence.

As they grew and learned to walk, life became like it had been when we first arrived at the sea; the girls, these two lovely olive nymphs, brought us back to lives long forgotten. We stood on the shore and watched the sun rise. We went for long walks collecting feathers of different kinds of birds. We slept outside, letting the starlight drizzle over us; Atara and Yaffa curled between Eve and me, their faces softly lit by moonlight.

Eve and I saw everything anew with them.

"Those are stars," I said.

"Tar," said Atara.

"No, starrrr," said Yaffa.

Atara looked over at me. "You made the stars?"

"No, my sweet girl, The Maker made them. He made the moon, too, and all that you see."

I watched their eyes move back and forth across the night sky. There was so much these two little girls didn't know. Even then I remember thinking there was so much of our story to tell our daughters, somehow, someday. For the story had become their family history.

During the day we walked with them, hand in hand, and taught them to swim, holding them as they kicked, their long black hair floating around them as they bobbed in the sea. I taught them to jump and then dive from one of the rocks that sat further out in the water, off the beach.

Eve bathed them in the bathing pool and put bellflower

oil on them. She tied flowers around their wrists. I taught them to milk a goat and Eve taught them to search for quail eggs.

We were a family again. And for a long time I did not travel up the coast and fish for days at a time as I had done in the past.

The girls were occupied chasing a squirrel in the vineyard. The squirrel was in no danger. It was mid-afternoon and I was wearing only my inner wrap. I had moved out of the hot sun into the shade of the storehouse. A light breeze found its way to me as I was thinking of taking a break and going for a short swim. Just then Eve walked up, past me, and into the storehouse. I followed her in to see what it was she was after.

Without a word, she took me. She came to me as if we were still young, perfect creatures. Dried mint and chamomile hung above us, the scent of it wafted, like dust in the shafts of sunlight that came through the slats in the walls. She stripped her clothes, then mine, with such grace and desire. She was the mother of all living. She put her trust in the promise of our numbers, our future was hers to make. So she came to me and there in the cool shade she stretched herself over me, the warm breeze flowing across my legs, up her back, and into the rafters.

In the harvest, just as the sea was beckoning to me once again, Seth was born. With light-colored, very fine hair and delicate features, he became the center of our family. He was the one we talked to and talked about. He learned to walk with his arms stretched, his hands held by his two older sisters. We could see the mothers in our daughters as they cared for this boy, cuddling with him around the fire or wading with him at the edge of the sea.

One morning we heard a sound coming from Seth's sleeping loft. It was like he was trying to speak, but only long sounds came out. The sounds slurred up and down. We all went and gathered around him. He was awake. He was making this sound in his mouth, but his lips were closed. He was humming. It was through Seth we realized we could sing.

I began to teach Seth all I taught my other two sons, yet I also began to have trouble carrying on life at home. I felt pent up in this house that had grown small with the children. Eve told each of them what to do, giving them tasks each morning. I followed them around doing what I could but I was restless.

Time passed, seasons came and went, and routines were established. Eve and I spoke little more than a word to each other. She focused on the children.

At my suggestion we began to offer a sacrifice for the family each evening, but it felt like we were performing a play, the two of us standing in front of the altar, the flames flinging sparks into the dusk air as the children stood off in the shadows, unsure what we were trying to show them. We had become a pair of strangers with shared memories.

I often left early in the morning and returned late in the evening or even the next day, going over and over into the wild and leaving the order of home to Eve, for she had it well in hand.

"Eve, I think I will go on one of my hunts tomorrow."

"Go ahead."

"I think I may be gone for several days."

"The sun will rise and set without you."

Seth came over to me and sat down on my knee. He was in that stage between boy and man, the tips of his toes touched the floor. I hadn't known he was in the room as I told Eve I was leaving, but he looked at me and I could see in his eyes the space I was creating by not being here. But he said nothing, and I offered less as I gathered my travelsack and wandered off.

I returned three days and nights later with a net full of all manner of sea creature, as well as the better fruit and vegetable specimens I had spotted along the way. Many of these could not be found where we lived near the sea.

"How are you, stranger of mine?" she asked with a smile meeting me at the door.

"I have not returned with my hands empty," I said.

She looked at me. Past the smile I could see the distance in her eyes. "You are still Adam of Eden, aren't you? Tamer of all Creation."

She said this as if what I had been doing was child's play, as if I were playing a character I'd invented.

I unpacked the goods, explaining what I had seen, how I had been nearly buried alive by the waves from a strong wind, forced deep into the land. "I saw herds of horses, like none I've seen before," I said. "My horse stopped and called to them, sniffing the air of their stampede."

She said nothing more.

We spent the next several evenings cooking, adding spices at different times and in combinations.

One of those evenings we had a large pot simmering and had just added a few seeds and flakes. As the spices rolled in the broth and sea meat, we both leaned in at the same time to smell the steam. Our foreheads touched. In silence we stayed like this for a few brief moments. It seemed possible at that moment, the cookery a delightful mess, Seth lying on the floor with a kitten, Atara and Yaffa watching him, to reclaim ourselves; to become not just Adam or Eve, but Adam and Eve again.

"It seems perfect to me," I finally said, placing my hand on her back and breathing deep. I spoke of the broth, but I spoke more of the moment, with her.

"We need more water," she said as she turned away.

I remained there over the pot, the steam forming a layer of dew on my chin. It was in that scene, in that evening, I saw her and me. We were losing each other. We had learned how to live without each other.

She stood staring at me with a clay pitcher of water in her hand, waiting for me to move.

As Seth grew older he joined me on a trip now and then. My trips became longer and I began exploring by sea. I had built rafts by felling trees and strapping them together with hemp. These rafts, once I learned to control them using a long thin plank, allowed me to skirt the shore for weeks, seeing what I wished of the farthest shore.

It was during this time, when I was home between travels, that one evening after dinner one of the girls, I don't remember which and it isn't important (for it could have been either of them and changed nothing), heard me mention that I was going for a walk. She wanted to join me.

"Yes. That would be wonderful," I said.

We began to ready ourselves for a hike up the north shore. The girls had become young women by now; she certainly didn't need my help getting ready. She was old enough to take the walk alone.

Eve walked in and asked me what we were doing.

"A hike," I said a bit too loudly and with a tone as if it should be obvious.

Eve heard and stepped between me and our daughter, who was standing, ready, with her hat in her hand. "No." Eve took our daughter's empty hand and began to lead her through the cookhouse and toward the garden.

"It is such a lovely evening. You should join us!" I called as I followed along behind.

Eve stopped, turned and looked at me with condemnation and disgust. "No, you can go alone. Why don't you take the vine with you instead?" She said nothing more, continuing toward the door.

With a slow lumbering swat, I grabbed at the girl as she walked behind Eve. Eve pulled her close and both of them stepped easily out of my reach. But I had gone too far and was past the tips of my toes. My balance left me. I fell forward, twisting to the side in an attempt to avoid a heavy wooden table we had sitting just inside the garden door. Down I went, the side of my head catching the corner of the table just above and to the outside of my right eye.

I woke on the floor where I had fallen, my shoulder resting against the leg of the table. The house was quiet, the sun nearly set. A clean, dark-blue light filled the windows. I lay there on the floor with the worst headache ever had by man or beast. Through the fog of pain and humiliation of being left there on the floor, I knew I needed to leave.

I needed to go out and away for good.

Oren of Susa: On Leaving

Within the next two days I will take my leave. I will travel the road toward home. I will take with me all I brought, as well as a jar of sea water, a coat made of fur, and the manuscript. All of these items belong to me except the last. I would leave it behind but Adam has asked me to have a copy made of the story.

"I will have Amat do it. I trust him to do it well." Of course it will satisfy his curiosity and he and I can then talk together about it as well.

"I'll send Mahesh to get them from you," said Adam.

As always I will pick fruit to eat as I travel. But this time I will look at the fruit growing from the tree and I will pause. For I will be carrying with me the memory of a story told, of animals and angels, a serpent and a great tree, the love of a woman, the loss of children, and The Maker of it all.

I will leave because I will be finished writing. I have completed the work. Adam has offered to take me to the home — the place where he and Eve lived — to see the field where Abel is buried.

"The house is still there, deeply worn but standing."

But I told him no. "Let's make that a trip for the future." I want to get back to Susa. I want to see Teel. Besides, this is an offer Adam can't fulfill. Such a trip happens only in his imagination. For I am sure the next time he leaves his bed will be when his servants hoist his still and silent body from upon it.

Susa will look different to me — the messengers, the bathers, the crowds in the marketplace, and the wide dirt streets. This story has formed a glass before my eye, a pane through which I will always look.

And the next time I go to bathe I will look up and I will see the gods of Susa on their poles. I will see their sightless eyes, their deaf ears, their throats that pass no sound.

And I may be thought a fool, but I will know.

And I will tell my son and my grandson.

Men may make gods, but there is a Maker of men. And The Maker sees, and there are actions The Maker takes in this world of sun and wind.

For The Maker's hands are not still, they move.

Yet turned away are the heads and distracted are the minds of men.

Chapter Fourteen

How to Hold a Remnant

I'd found a spot most of a day's journey up the shore and I had constructed what would become the start of my new home, the home I have to this day. I was spending much of the season on this finger of land with the sea all around me. I continued my visits to see her. Within the next three harvests three more children were born to us—a girl, a boy, and a girl, the last of our children. These were named Urlah, Bish, and Mevlah.

Once every season I returned south to Eve's, sometimes staying for several moons in a row to visit the children. On some of my visits Seth would come from his home further south to see me. I became the visitor-father, a friendly fisherman and farmer. My cart was loaded down as I came up the path I had worn, always bringing enough food and supply to last until my next appearance.

"How are you?" she would say as she helped me unload the goods—meats I had dried or salted, vegetables, firewood. The children, too, would help, the youngest reaching up and pulling themselves onto the back of the cart.

"Well enough. A wind storm crossed the point two nights past. I will have the roof repaired by the new moon." I spoke of things, not of thoughts.

I wondered what reason she had to be pleased with my safety. Of course we were unloading the cart I had packed early that day, so that was one reason. But I think she had some true care for me. I think there was some small, hot ember of memory and love between us which we were both drawn close to at times, like nomads to a fire at night on an open plain. We still had a reference point, a place we both once knew, a common landmark which had once held our youthful attention and had come now to hold a remnant of our graying souls.

So I came back, over and over. I watched the children grow and I did what I could for them in their early years. I dutifully taught fishing and planting to all of them. I taught Bish to build a house and a raft. I came for seasons and seasons more.

One midsummer visit I drew to within sight of the house. My cart loaded down, the morning sun casting my shadow long and thin toward the trees. As I drew closer to the house no one came out. No one came down the path to see me and my loaded cart.

I rolled to a stop at the base of the path up to the door and listened to the silence of my wheels, the breathing of the horse and the insects in the tall grass. The sea fell on the beach in long, soft breaks. The breeze was perfectly warmed and made a faint whistle as it rustled the grass. I had left in the moonlight and traveled through the early hours, into the dawn.

As I sat there atop my cart and looked around me, I knew.

They were gone.

I stepped down from my cart.

The vineyard struggled under the weeds towering over the trellises. The stack of Abel's rocks, his last effort, had thin moss covering it. I wondered if the other children knew what the stack of rocks meant. The door of the house hung open, swinging slightly with the breeze.

I walked inside.

I was right. The house was empty, save for only a few clay jars tipped over in one corner. Though I didn't have this image for it then, it was as if I was staring into a burial cave which had been robbed. The emptiness, the clearing was complete. I went to stand up the jars and found one of them was cracked.

I took it down to the cart and bound it tight with some hemp I had brought along. I tried to repair it, to fix it, to make it right again. I stood it back in place, in the corner again, but it looked disturbed, the dirt on it smudged and rearranged, the hemp making it different than all the others, as if it had just joined the other jars after a journey from a faraway place.

The children were getting older. Even the last of them was only several years from being grown, yet I thought she would stay. I couldn't imagine her anywhere else. We had not talked about it, but I thought she would remain there at that house. She knew I would come again. She knew I would find this, this empty house here by the sea.

Not knowing what else to do, I unloaded what I'd brought for them: two large, salted fishes, a squash, a few leeks, a head of cabbage, and three stacks of firewood. I set these next to the jars. Maybe she would come and take these things. Maybe I would come again and bring more and see if these were gone.

Maybe the distance was too much for either of us now.

Back outside I latched the door. I paused and felt the smooth wooden handle. I remembered setting that handle, a simple wooden peg set at a downward angle. I saw that the grass on the corner of the roof was lifted up, pulling away from the house. Fetching the rest of the hemp I lashed the grass tight again and tied it off. I walked through the tall grass and stepped into the vineyard. I cleared the overgrowth from the first grape vine. Several clusters of the fruit hung underneath. The morning sun now reached their purple skins. Finally, I brushed clear the sand from the stone path, stone by stone, down to my empty cart.

I climbed back up and took the tethers of the horse in the palms of my dirty hands. I had done the last of what I could do for her, for them.

I was again alone. A deep desire for the past set in, a heartsickness for what once was. Any time in the past was better than right now. It had always been that she stood with me in my regret, with me and against it, but she was on the other side now. She was part of it. In leaving she had become part of the burden, part of the weight.

I didn't know it then, but I would see her again one day. I would stand at her bedside and look upon her once more.

I've been given a long life since that day. I am an ancient and wealthy man. My first grandson, Enosh, lives here near me part of the season. He is himself an old man, but he is a master of records and tracks my field and sea trade, reaping the profits along with me. He spends one day a week at the market, delivering goods to the shop we have there.

Settlements have sprung up all along the coast road toward the village. The market there thrives, drawing from all the inland settlements in the region and beyond. Indeed, my descendants, the families of my children's grandest grandchildren are too many for me to count, even in a hundred sleepless moons. They are many, and I am but one.

There is a servant who aides Enosh and works the stable. Have you seen him—a thin, muscled, young man with loose, curly hair? I don't know his name nor do I know his lineage, but he has a small garden plot outside his cottage, at the edge of my land. There he stands up a great variety of plants in rows and studies them in their place, marveling in their ways. And he has with him a beautiful young woman. The curious, youthful servant has taken her as his wife. She is always at his side. She is a helper and a mate to him. The servant delights in her, and they lay together in the evenings by the sea.

And this young servant, he believes. He believes that she has been given to him, that she is a gift from The Maker.

Acknowledgments & Gratitudes

There have been many, many times that I wondered why no one beat me to this project, a literary orthodox retelling of this narrative. I feel like God left this wonderful gift on the floor of the forest, just off the path, for me to stumble upon. I'm deeply thankful for the book of Genesis—the truth of our origins made available in simple words. I am grateful for the scholars who have learned Hebrew and this literature, and written their translations and scholarly understanding for people like me to read. Among these are Bruce Waltke, Robert Alter, Lawrence Turner, and Eugene Peterson.

Every debut novel has a unique journey. This one has been no different. The eyewitnesses have been many—hundreds of conversations and hundreds of friendships spanning fifteen years. For this reason, these are the hardest pages in a novel to write.

To Jack Musgrave: You taught my senior English class at Warsaw High School, Warsaw, IN. You told us to read Vonnegut. I started there and never looked back. Writers are readers first. I have a hunch that you knew that.

This novel found its way during the five years I spent in the MFA at Butler University in Indianapolis. After long days at the office I walked into fiction workshops that proved nothing less than transformative to my creative work.

To Dan Barden, Michael Dahlie, Micah Ling, Allison Lynn, and Greg Schwipps: To sit in your workshops was both an education and a delight. Thank you, Mindy Dunn, for all you do for our MFA community and for reading my thesis simply because you wanted to. The temptation to try to name all my colleagues over the years at Butler is unbearable, yet the fear of failing at such a task wins out.

To my peer MFA poets: I stood at the periphery and soaked up your sensibilities. I listened to your readings and I watched your ways. I trust you'll see your influence on my prose.

To my peer MFA nonfiction writers: I was so often the happy recipient of your interest in the mysteries of fiction. Your support and friendship was my earliest in the program.

To my fellow MFA fiction writers: You saw this manuscript when it was ugly and you suggested that it could be otherwise. You collectively produced hundreds of pages of workshop notes. I still have every one of them—organized by course in a filing cabinet next to my workbench in the garage. How will I write my second novel without you?

To Hilene Flanzbaum: The course on Midrash was certainly timely, wasn't it! You later agreed to be my thesis reader. You brought unfailing belief, expertise, and sensibilities—in equal parts.

To Ben H. Winters: You welcomed my request to advise my thesis at Butler. You supported this project in person, via phone, via email, and over brunch at Le Peep off 71st Street. And you offered to write Jöelle Delbourgo, your literary agent, with an introduction.

To Jöelle: You loved this manuscript from the start. You believed in its future even as my belief faltered. Your experience, advising, coaching, and guidance are gifts I hope to never be without. Thank you for lunch al fresco in Montclair, NJ at Raymonds on November 3, 2017. Let's do that again. This time it's on me.

To George and Karen Porter: I'll never forget our meeting on August 4, 2018 at the Professional Writers' Conference at Taylor University. You listened to me talk about Adam and Oren, and with open minds you read the first 35 pages. Soon you welcomed me into the Bold Vision fold.

To the team at Bold Vision, editor Lindsay Franklin, and artist Maddie Scott: Thank you for your many contributions, always with care and with creative energy.

To Scott Carter, my social media consultant, technician, and friend: Thank you for stepping in when I most needed your expertise and approaching the effort with professionalism, creativity, and enthusiasm.

To Warren Burns, Darrell and Wendi Campbell, Pat and Melissa Denton, Neil and Marcia Denton, Jim and Amy

Knapp, Mark and Michelle Lamb, and Amber Troyer: Thank you for reading earlier drafts of this manuscript and for the notes and conversations that influenced each draft thereafter.

Thank you to the founding members of the Westside Writers' Workshop: Teresa Fales, Jim Knapp, Rita O'Riley, and Roger Shuman. With you I will write my second novel. The Beehive in Danville awaits our next meeting even as Andrea Shuman writes by the very best Light.

Julia, Lydia, and Tate: You are my legacy, not this book. Nor any book. Thank you for sharing your childhoods with Adam of Eden. I love you.

And this spot on this page is reserved for Cyndi. You spent as many hours alone as I did. You read the first paragraph of the first draft. Only you and I have done that. And you, to the benefit of all involved, read everything that leaves my desk. Thank you for sharing life with me. This book is yours as much as it's mine. All my love.

Meet the Author

David J. Marsh

Dave came to belief as a child and grew up steeped in biblical narratives. His mother read to him and his father was a pastor as well as a student of both theology and biblical languages.

Growing up, Dave often asked his father to read aloud the scriptures in their original Hebrew and Greek. While Dave could not understand them, the music of these languages in their original tongue fascinated him. His father's library of commentaries now lines a wall in his home.

In his debut novel, *The Confessions of Adam*, a re-telling of the universal and dramatic narrative that opens the book of Genesis, he has crafted a richly imagined story of creation and its aftermath—drawing on a lifetime of familiarity with the text as well as more recent study.

David J. Marsh holds a BS in Communications from Grace College, Winona Lake, IN and an MFA in Creative Writing from Butler University, Indianapolis. Dave's work has been recognized by or appeared in *Utmost, Booth Online, NoiseMedium,* and *Fixional.*

Dave facilitates the Westside Writers' Workshop and twice monthly he posts a column on the craft of fiction called "Revel and Rant" at www.davidjmarsh.com.

Please join Dave on
instagram at davidjmarshauthor
Twitter @marshjdavid
Facebook @DavidJMarshAuthor

Dave and his wife Cyndi reside in Danville, Indiana.